LET ME IN
30 TALES OF TERROR

TALES OF TERROR
BOOK FOUR

BLAIR DANIELS

By Blair Daniels
Copyright © 2024 Blair Daniels
All rights reserved.

Black Widow Press
http://www.blairdaniels.com

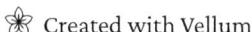 Created with Vellum

CONTENTS

The Camera That Shows Your Last Photograph	1
Skinwalkers Are Staying At My Motel	10
Chores	29
Always Check For Your Shadow	34
Be Careful What Your Kids Watch on YouTube	42
The Strange Grocery Store	52
There's Something Wrong With The Moon	71
Monster In Your Closet	75
Has Anyone Heard Of The Bloodworth Incident?	77
Strange Dog	86
Disturbing Youtube Ad	104
The Headless Jogger	112
I Hacked A Ring Camera	118
Garden Hose	123
There's Something Wrong With This Hospital	130
A Phone Call With My Husband	150
I Let Something Into My House	153
This Is My House	159
I Hear Someone Walking Beside Me Every Night	162
My Daughter	167
A Pyramid Scheme For The Dark Lord	170
The Lake Is Not Wet	177
I Hear Voices	180
The Zmory	183
Minecraft	188
Mail-Order Husband	193

My Husband Wears People's Faces	199
I'm Trapped In An Infinite Suburb	205
I Deliver Letters To Dead People	218
The Cursed House	238
Inspiration Behind the Stories	243
Also by Blair Daniels	247

The charm of horror only tempts the strong.

— JEAN LORRAIN

THE CAMERA THAT SHOWS YOUR LAST PHOTOGRAPH

Everyone dies at some point.

And with that reality come some cold, hard facts. You will have a last kiss. A last hug. A last phone call. And... a last photograph.

On Friday night, we met up at Casey's house. Even though she has an annoying neighbor, her parents built this amazing fire pit that's the perfect spot for chilly autumn nights. After starting the fire and roasting some marshmallows, she brought out something I hadn't seen in at least a decade: a disposable camera.

"This is a special camera," Casey said, with a grin. "Apparently, when you take a picture... it'll be your last photo before you die."

I sat there, trying to digest what she was saying. "You mean... the camera kills you?"

"Yeah, like that one Goosebumps book," Brady replied.

"Say Cheese and Die! Oh my gosh, I *loooved* that one!" Maribel said, grinning.

"Nonono, that's not what I mean." Casey held her hands up, clearly annoyed that we didn't get it. "Everyone has a last photo before they die. Like, for example, my grandpa... Three days before he passed away, he went on a fishing trip. The last photo on that trip... is the last photo that was ever taken of him."

"Well, it's impossible for a camera to show that," I replied. "It would have to be a time-traveling camera for that to work."

"You guys are no fun!" Casey rolled her eyes and started putting the camera back in her bag.

"Wait, wait. We didn't say we didn't want to use it," Maribel said.

"Yeah. It could be fun," I added.

A wicked smile flashed on Casey's lips. "Okay. Good. Who wants to be the first?"

Brady raised his hand. "I'll go."

That was Brady for you. Never missed a chance to impress the girls. He stood up, his face lit by the roaring fire. "Where should I stand?"

"The lighting's kinda harsh. Maybe by that tree."

Brady walked several feet away from the fire and stood next to the tree. Then he leaned against it, crossed his arms, and raised an eyebrow.

Casey raised the camera to her face. "3, 2, 1... cheese!"

Click.

White light flashed across the dark backyard.

Brady stepped away from the tree, grinning. "Okay, who's next?" Casey asked.

"I'll go," Maribel said.

She pushed her glasses up her nose and stood next to the tree, somewhat awkwardly. Casey lifted the camera to her face again and took a photo.

Click.

The ratcheting sound of her rewinding the film filled the air. "Okay, Benny, your turn," she said, shooting me a smile.

I walked over to the tree, took off my baseball cap, and waited. Casey lifted the camera to her face, then frowned. "Can't you smile?"

"Nope."

"Ugh. Fine."

Click.

She rewound the film and handed the camera to me. Then she posed next to the tree, in a classic sorority-squat pose.

Yeah, this wasn't awkward at all.

Casey and I had just started dating. But the longer things went on, the more doubts I was having. Sure, we looked good in pictures: a classic football star/cheerleader match. In reality, we weren't either of those things. She was pretty, but extremely insecure, jealous, and high maintenance. I was a neurodivergent math nerd who just happened to luck out genetically and look like a jock.

I stared at her through the viewfinder, her form slightly distorted.

Click.

"Hey, you didn't count down!" she whined.

"What? You were posing."

"I want to know *exactly* when the photo is being taken. That's all."

"Okay. Sure."

I rewound the camera and handed it back to her. She sidled up next to me and lowered her voice. "Hey, when Brady and Maribel leave… you want to stay a little bit after?"

"Oh… I don't know. My dad's renovating the kitchen, and he wants me to help him in the morning—"

"It doesn't have to be long. Just for a little while."

I should've said no. But she was pushing, and I felt bad saying no. "Okay. Just for a half hour."

"Sounds good to me. We can watch something down in the basement. My parents can't hear a thing down there."

"What about your neighbor? He seemed really mad when we were watching *V for Vendetta*. Said the explosions woke him up. Remember, he was pounding on the glass door and yelling at us?"

She rolled her eyes. "So we'll keep the volume down. Come on, it's just a half hour. We don't even have to watch anything."

"… Okay."

Before I could say more, she grabbed the camera and started towards the fire pit. I followed. "When are you gonna get those developed?" Brady asked.

"We could go tonight. There's still a 1-hour photo

in the CVS on Route 14," Maribel replied. "And we could pick up some snacks."

"Wait, seriously? They still develop photos?" Casey asked.

"Mm-hmm. My dad uses them for like, passport photos and other official stuff."

So it was decided.

The four of us piled into Brady's car and took off into the night.

We spent the entire hour hanging out at the store, picking out snacks. Then Casey went up to the counter, grabbed the paper envelope, and led us back out to the car. We piled inside and Brady turned on the lights.

She flicked open the envelope and pulled out the photos.

"No fucking way."

The first photo showed an older man standing on a beach. Gray hair dripping wet, blue waves rolling behind him. But with his square jaw and tall build, he looked just like an aged-up Brady.

"That's impossible," I said.

"Not necessarily," Maribel replied, after a pause. "The camera *looked* like a disposable camera, but it's possible someone put a cheap microchip in there. Like a mini Raspberry Pi, or something. Then it took our photos, and with the help of AI, aged them up."

"Yeah but, how would the CVS develop them?" I asked.

"Maybe it was straightforward. Maybe when he opened the camera to get the film, there was a USB stick there instead, loaded up with the images. So he just stuck it in the computer and printed them out. It's weird, but... Amazon is full of weird shit like this. I once saw a karaoke machine that used AI to autotune everyone as they were singing, in real time."

"We could go back inside and ask them," I suggested.

"I want to see the rest of the photos first," Casey said, nearly cutting me off.

"Where'd you get this camera, again?" Maribel asked.

"A friend gave it to me."

And with that vague response, she flipped to the next photo.

It was a family Christmas photo. Several people standing in front of the tree, happy faces lit by multi-colored lights.

But my heart dropped when I saw the woman on the left.

A woman, maybe 30. Holding a little baby. With the same heart-shaped face, the same curly dark hair as Maribel.

"Oh no," she said, her eyes wide.

We all stared at the photo, silently, unsure what to say.

But then I saw it. In the middle of the photo, sitting on the couch, was an old woman. A *very* old woman, with skin so wrinkled it looked like crepe paper, and hair so white it looked like a tuft of cotton candy on her head.

Wire-framed glasses were perched on her nose.

"I think *that's* you."

Maribel snatched the photo out of Casey's hands. "Woah," she whispered, studying it up close.

For all her big talk about this being some AI thing, she seemed to take it pretty seriously.

As I watched Maribel, I couldn't help but smile. For a second, I felt something—a sense of awe as I looked at her face, lighting up with the joy of her family. I'd never looked at Maribel as anything other than a friend, but there was something tugging at my heartstrings now. Not even something I could put into words as a crush, or attraction, or lust— just *something*. A flicker of connection, of emotion, of—

"... Benny?"

I glanced at Casey.

And then I looked down.

In her hands was the photo she'd taken of me.

The exact same photo. Of me, tonight, holding my baseball cap, standing next to the tree. Not smiling. Staring straight ahead, eyes red from the flash.

My first thought was the camera had malfunctioned. Whatever this was, AI or otherwise, had messed up and glitched on my picture. And it just spit out the photo as it was taken tonight.

But as Casey, Brady, and Maribel stared at me with horror, I realized.

"So it's saying... the picture you took of me, tonight... is the last picture of me alive."

"I guess so," Casey said.

The silence pressed in. I shook my head and forced a laugh. "Come on, this is just some stupid prank camera. Like Maribel said, it's some AI thing. Maybe it even purposely skips some people to scare them."

None of them were laughing.

"Okay, come on, let's look at Casey's."

I plucked my photo from the stack—

And froze.

Casey was sitting on the floor of someone's basement.

Her hands were tied to a metal support pole with thick rope. A strip of duct tape had been placed over her mouth. The left side of her head was matted with blood, and a thin trail dripped down the side of her face. Her blue eyes were wide with fear—

And looking straight at whoever was taking the photo.

"This is some sick fucking prank," Brady muttered, his voice low with anger.

Casey just sat there, frozen.

"Let's go home," Maribel said. "Forget about all this stuff. It's just... a prank... like Brady said."

But Casey didn't move. She just sat there, the photo shaking in her hands. Her blue eyes wide with fear.

"What's wrong?" Maribel asked, softly.

"The basement..." she said, finally, pointing at the

photo. "I recognize it. My dad and I went over there one time when he needed help with the fuse box and I —I thought he was annoying but I never—"

"Casey. Whose basement is it?" I asked.

She looked up at me, her eyes wide.

"My neighbor's."

SKINWALKERS ARE STAYING AT MY MOTEL

If you're ever driving down Route 106 in Michigan, and you see a sign for the Greenbriar Motel, you better just keep on driving. Because there is something terribly wrong here, and the last thing I would want is for more people to die.

I started working at the Greenbriar Motel a week ago. It wasn't a dream job by any standards: night shift at the front desk, checking people in and out, doing some inventory in the back. I liked the peace and quiet, though: as a little rundown motel on a stretch of isolated highway in Michigan, it gave me a lot of time to read and play computer games on the clock. It also helped that the owner, Frank, didn't seem to care I was a high school dropout with a rap sheet.

But on the very first day, I felt that something was terribly off.

For one, there was the smell. When the wind

shifted, the entire parking lot smelled like rotting meat. I ran to close the windows, but even then I could still smell it, seeping in through the HVAC system. The motel is surrounded by deep woods, so I figured maybe we were near the kill grounds of some animal. Or maybe it was just the endless roadkill of deer and possums on the highway.

Either way, it was unsettling. And definitely not enjoyable.

The other thing that struck me as odd were the guests' rooms. Some of them didn't have windows—and it seemed like that was intentional. I could see the lines in the paint, the seams outlining where windows had once been. When I asked Frank, he told me that some of the guests asked for windowless rooms. That they were in high demand. He didn't elaborate, and honestly, I was a little scared to press him on it.

Things went from strange to downright creepy, however, as soon as Frank left. As I got set up at my desk, a woman walked into the room.

She was in her 40s, maybe, with black hair and very pale skin. As soon as she stepped inside, she locked the door behind her. "Frank left, right?" she asked me.

"Yeah," I replied. "Uh... who are you?"

She introduced herself as Matilda. She'd been working here for a decade, cleaning the motel rooms after the guests checked out. After a few minutes of small talk, she suddenly came up to the counter and lowered her voice.

"I want to make sure you're safe around here," she said, glancing back towards the door nervously. "So I need you to listen to me. Okay?"

My heart dropped. "Uh... okay?"

"Whatever you do, don't ask questions. Just check people in, check them out, and mind your own business. And then, you'll be fine."

My stomach did a little flip. Okay, so it was *that* kind of motel. Illegal business of multiple kinds, probably, all being conducted under our dilapidated roof. "What... what if the police come? Will I be arrested, too?"

She gave me a blank stare. "The police?"

"Say they find... evidence of illegal activity in one of the rooms. Will that get me in trouble? I already have shoplifting on my record and can't—"

She shook her head. "Don't worry about the police. Just don't ask questions. And don't make eye contact, or look at their faces for too long."

I swallowed. *They don't want witnesses. They don't want me to be able to pick them out of a lineup,* I thought. "Okay. I won't ask questions, and I won't look at them for too long. Got it."

She smiled at me. "You have nothing to worry about."

As it turned out, though, I had quite a lot to worry about.

That night, I checked in three people. They were almost like caricatures: a big, strong guy in sunglasses that looked like he'd stepped right out of *The Godfather*. A woman dressed to the 9s, wearing a more makeup than a clown. A skinny young guy in a hoodie that smelled of something chemical and strange.

But I listened to Matilda. I didn't ask questions. I didn't even ask the questions I should've been asking—like when Hoodie Guy gave me an ID that was clearly fake. *Don't ask questions and you'll be fine.* I kept repeating that to myself. And I kept my eyes glued to the computer screen, never even glancing up at them.

When it hit midnight, I assumed the rest of the night would be smooth sailing. On this lonely stretch of highway, it was unlikely anyone else would check in. I pulled up *Minesweeper* and played some music on my phone.

My peace and quiet, however, was interrupted by the door swinging open. At 2 AM.

I glanced up to see the guy in sunglasses—the guy who looked like he'd stepped out of *The Godfather.*

Oh, no. I should've locked the door... I swallowed and kept my eyes glued to the computer screen as he approached. "Can I help you?" I asked, watching him in my peripheral vision.

"Do you have any razors for purchase?"

I froze. *Razors? At 2 AM?* I instantly got a mental image of him slashing someone up in his room. Blood all over the sheets, soaking into the carpet. "Uh, no, we don't have any razors," I said, keeping my eyes on the computer screen.

"Can you just check in the back, please?"

I swallowed. I really, *really* didn't want to go check. As soon as I turned around, he could do anything. Pull out a gun. Tackle me. Force me into a chokehold and keep me hostage.

But refusing him was just as bad, if not worse. It might make him mad. *Really* mad.

I sat there, staring at *Minesweeper* on the screen, weighing my options. Paying close attention to him out of the corner of my eye.

And that's when I saw it.

There was something… off… about this guy. His sunglasses looked like they were slightly too low on his face. Like the eyes they were covering weren't in quite the right place. And not only that, but I couldn't see his eyebrows poking above the frames, or the contours of his brow ridge. Everything above the glasses was perfectly flat and smooth. Like he had no eye sockets at all.

"Can you check in the back, please?" he asked again, his voice taking on an annoyed tone.

"Y-yes. Sure."

I sprung out of the seat and ducked into the back storage area. I quickly glanced over my shoulder to make sure he wasn't following me—but he wasn't. I had half a mind to just stay there, hiding out in the back storage room, until I heard his voice calling me.

"Did you find them?"

He sounded angry. Approaching furious.

Thankfully, I *did* find a few packaged razors next to some spare toothbrushes and soap we kept. I grabbed them and handed them over, keeping my eyes trained on the floor. "Thank you," he said, sounding pleased.

And that was it. He turned around and left.

As soon as the door shut, I ran over and locked it. I closed the blinds and sat back down at the front desk, my heart hammering in my chest. All I could picture were the strange contours of his face.

And as I sat there, I realized something. All three guests that I'd checked in since the start of my shift—the Godfather guy, the Makeup woman, the Hoodie guy—had something covering their face or head. I mean, I wasn't exaggerating about the woman having enough makeup for a clown. She was wearing foundation so thick that it cracked around the corners of her eyes and lips, and wore false eyelashes so long they gave the appearance of spider legs. And Hoodie Guy had kept his hood pulled so tightly over his head that his ears and hair weren't visible.

It was like they all had something to hide.

Morning couldn't come soon enough. As soon as the day shift workers arrived, I got the hell out of there. I floored it back to my house and slept for a long time, my sleep plagued with nightmares of faceless people and spidery eyelashes.

Then it was time to go back to the motel for night #2.

Thankfully, it was a quieter night. Although the VACANCY sign glowed brightly in the darkness, no one checked in during my shift. They must've all come earlier, during the day shift. I locked the door, sat down with a cup of coffee, and enjoyed getting some reading done in the quiet.

Unfortunately, the quiet didn't last long. Around midnight, I heard a loud *slam* from outside.

I threw my book down and ran over to the window.

The door to room 16 was wide open.

I looked around. Nobody appeared to be outside; the parking lot, and the sidewalk, were empty. The room itself was dark—none of the lights were on.

I walked over to the computer and looked up the room. To my surprise, no one had booked it for tonight.

Should I go out and close the door?

I hesitated. It was late. There was no one around, except for the occasional passing car. If someone had broken into that room... and then attacked me... there would be no one to hear me scream.

So I kept the door locked tight and accessed the security camera feed instead. As I rewound it, I saw what happened: the door had opened, and then a woman had walked out of it. I couldn't see her face— just her long dark hair.

She then disappeared into room 22.

I checked room 22 on the computer, and saw it was booked to a woman named Cassandra Johnson.

I frowned. Looked like Cassandra might be going into our vacant rooms and possibly stealing stuff. Matilda must've forgotten to lock up the room after she cleaned it. I sighed, opened the door, and began walking towards the open room.

I thought of knocking on room 22, but then thought better of it. *Keep your nose out of other people's business*. I'd just lock up room 16 and go back to the lobby, like a good little employee.

I walked towards to the open room. But as soon as I got close, a horrible smell wafted out of the room. Like something rotting, decaying. My stomach turned. What did Cassandra do in there? Throw up? Stash all her garbage in there?

I reached into the darkness of the room. Bracing myself, I flicked on the light.

The room looked normal. The bed was made. The carpet was clean. But the smell had only intensified. I pinched my nose as I glanced around, starting to feel nauseous.

And then I saw it.

There was... something... on the carpet. Just barely poking out from the other side of the bed.

What *is* that? It was tan, and folded over itself. Like a beige sheet or pillowcase had been bunched up on the other side. But all our sheets were white. I stepped into the room, my heart pounding in my chest. "Hello?" I called out.

Nothing.

The smell got even worse as I approached the bed. Nausea washed over me. I forced myself to keep going, pinching my nose, swallowing down the urge to throw up.

I peered over the side of the bed—and froze.

There was a pile of beige, slightly translucent material folded over itself on the other side. But I instantly recognized certain shapes attached to it. Awfully familiar shapes. Like five fingers, resembling a glove made of skin, poking out from under one of the folds.

It looked like someone had *shed their skin*.

I stepped back, my legs shaking underneath me. *Nonono. There's no way. It can't be...* I backed away, towards the door, my throat dry. Because it didn't make sense. It didn't even make sense with a horrible crime. There wasn't any blood on it. It hadn't been cut off someone. It was like a snake skin, clean and perfect, holding the shape of its wearer like a ghost.

I ran out of the room—

And saw, walking towards me down the sidewalk, the woman from room 22.

Strands of her dark, straight hair hung over her face. But I could tell, through her hair, that there was something wrong with her face—her eyes, her lips, were in *slightly* the wrong position. She strode towards me, fast, her shoes clicking on the pavement.

I didn't want to find out what she'd do if she caught me.

I whipped around and ran as fast as I could. I could hear her behind me, but I forced myself to go faster, and faster, until I was inside the lobby. I clicked the lock shut and collapsed in the back room, where she couldn't see me.

That's when the whistling started.

Just outside the door, I could hear her. Whistling. The source of the sound shifted as she circled the lobby area, looking for a way in. I heard it at the door. Then at the back. Then through the side windows. Then back at the front door.

This went on for an *hour*.

Finally, the whistling faded. But I didn't move. I stayed there, huddled in the back storage room, until dawn broke. As soon as the day shift arrived, I booked it out of there as fast as I could.

I wanted to quit. With everything I am, I wanted to just walk away.

But I needed the money. I already knew how hard it was, finding a job with a rap sheet. It was either go back to the job, or face eviction.

So I went back.

When I got on shift, though, I pulled Matilda aside and told her what I'd seen. I asked her again and again if my life was in danger. Asked her what the hell was going on here. If other people were in danger, too.

"I promise you. As long as you mind your own business, you'll be safe."

So that's what I did. I minded my own business. And for the next few days, nothing of note happened. Sure, there were a few people who checked in that were wearing hats or sunglasses or extra makeup, but I just tried to avoid eye contact with them. Tried to keep my head down and my nose out of other people's business.

But then came the night of November 14.

It was raining that night. The rain came down in sheets, and every so often, I heard a peal of thunder shake the windows. I wasn't expecting anyone to come in that night, as I hadn't seen that many cars driving by on the highway. The rain seemed to keep everybody in.

But then I heard a knock. When I looked up, I saw a man staring in the window.

A chill ran down my spine. He was wearing a hoodie that hid his head and kept his face mostly in shadow. And he was rather aggressively banging on the window—like he was in a hurry. I grabbed the mace I kept under the counter and slipped it into my pocket.

Then I approached the window.

"Do you have any vacancies?" he asked in a low voice, barely audible above the pounding rain.

The VACANCY sign glowed brightly behind him. There's no way he could've missed it.

"Yeah. Come on in," I said, unlocking the door with one hand and gripping the mace in my pocket with the other.

He stepped inside. Rain dripped off his jacket and onto the floor. I barely glanced at him, turning around and walking back around the counter. Then I sat down at the computer, keeping my eyes fixed on the screen.

In my peripheral vision, I could see him.

Leaning over the counter. His face only about a foot or two from mine. So close that I could smell the stale, mothball odor coming off his clothes. So close I could hear drops of water plopping onto the counter from his sleeve.

"Can you go faster?" he asked, his voice raspy in his throat.

"Sorry, sir—I'm going fast as I can," I replied, my heart starting to pound. "It's an old computer." My fingers slipped on the mouse as I rushed to click the buttons.

"I don't have all day," he growled, looming even closer to me.

I wanted to look at him. My eyes were itching to glance up at the man that was six inches from my face. But I forced myself to stare at the screen. Whatever the hell was going on here, I was not going to be a witness. I was not going to look up and find myself face-to-face with a Smith & Wesson.

"Your name?" I asked.

As soon as the words came out of my mouth, I froze. I needed a name to book the room. That's all. But maybe he wouldn't see it that way. Maybe I wasn't supposed to ask for names. Maybe that was part of Frank's understanding with certain guests.

Thankfully, nothing happened. After a second of hesitation, he replied, "Daniel Jones."

The name struck me as fake. Common first name, common last name. But who even cared at this point? I typed his name into the system and completed the booking process. He paid for the room in cash, which was another unnerving detail, but I tried not to worry about it. I turned my back and took a key off the hook. "Room 7," I said, handing it to him.

He thanked me, and then waited by the door.

I waited for a minute. Then two. But he didn't leave.

"Do you need something?" I asked, careful not to make eye contact.

"Can you escort me to my room?"

Oh, hell no.

There was no way I could go out there. In the middle of the night. With this creepy guy. That was like a death sentence. I glanced out the window and spotted his car—a beat-up sedan—in one of the nearby parking spaces.

The murder scenario played out in my head.

Shoves me into the hotel room.

Kills me.

Sticks my body in the trunk.

Throws it in the middle of the woods.

Or maybe worse. Maybe my skin would end up crumpled on the floor of one of the rooms. Maybe he'd take my form, or turn me into something that sheds its skin like a snake. That has eyes too low on its face. Or no eye sockets at all.

And the longer I looked at him, in the corner of my eye, the more I noticed how unsavory he looked. There were smears of dirt on his sleeves and on the hem of his pants. *Like he's been digging a grave,* the voice in my head added. His face, half-hidden in shadow, was sunken and gaunt. His jaw was covered in gray stubble, and his teeth were a horrible shade of grayish yellow.

"Can't... can't you just go yourself? I have something that I, uh, need to do here. My boss is going to be mad—"

"*You can take two minutes to walk me to my room, dammit!*"

I sat there in stunned silence. He sounded furious. My heart pounded in my ears. "Okay," I said, finally. My fingers curled around the mace in my pocket, and then I joined him by the door. "I'll walk you to your room."

He didn't thank me. He just grabbed the door and swung it open, nearly letting it swing back in my face.

I stepped out into the pouring rain with him. The parking lot was a lake, and our feet sloshed loudly through the water. The cold water seeped through my sneakers, and I shivered. I followed the man to his car, staying a good fifteen feet away. He popped the trunk, and I held my breath—but thankfully, there was only a duffel bag inside.

He hoisted it on his shoulder and started for Room 7. I followed him at a distance, staying several feet away, watching him fidget with the key.

"You got a lot of other people staying here right now?" he asked, as he slid the key into the lock.

"Some," I replied.

"Not great weather for it."

"Not really."

"The storm's supposed to clear tomorrow. It'll be good weather then."

Wow, this is taking a while, I thought to myself.

That's when I looked down at his hands—and noticed that he wasn't really *trying* to get into his room. He was just inserting the key, pausing, and then pulling it out. Over and over again.

He was stalling for time.

He was keeping me here, on purpose.

I looked up from his hands—just in time to see him staring at me. His blue eyes were intense, studying me.

I wanted to run away. Every inch of me was screaming to get out of there. But the guy had six inches on me, and was really thin—he'd probably catch me in seconds. I was never much of a runner.

I slipped my hand in my pocket, curling my fingers around the mace. "Do you need help getting into your room?" I asked.

He shook his head.

"I'm going to go back to the front desk," I said, taking a step back.

As soon as I said that, he froze. His eyes widened as he stared at me. Slowly, he shook his head, his lips stretching into a grimace that revealed his yellowed teeth.

"Don't go," he growled, his voice barely audible above the rain. "Stay exactly where you are."

I leapt into action. I whipped the mace out of my pocket and held it in front of me, pointing it right at him. "Don't get any closer!"

My finger hovered over the trigger—

And then I heard it.

Someone was whistling.

Behind me, somewhere in the rain. The song cut through the pattering raindrops like a knife.

It was the same eerie tune that woman had whistled a few days ago.

"I'm sorry," the man said quietly, his blue eyes locked on mine. "But I needed bait."

I stared at him. My brain couldn't even process what he was saying. *Bait?* I took a stumbling step back.

The whistling grew louder.

I whipped around. Through the rain, I could see someone walking through the parking lot. Barely lit by the flickering streetlamp. The mace fell from my hands and clattered to the ground.

Then I turned and ran as fast as I could towards the lobby.

The whistling stopped.

And then I could hear loud, splashing footsteps, growing louder with every second behind me—

I swung the door open, slammed it shut, and turned the lock. I pulled the blinds down over the window. Panting, I parted them with my fingertips and peered out into the night.

There was a woman standing in the parking lot.

The same woman I had seen a week ago.

Her hair and clothes were drenched with rain. But she was smiling—this big, lopsided grin that sent chills down my spine. And her eyes were strange, wide and wild, incredibly light blue. In the darkness, it almost looked like she didn't have irises at all. Just two pinholes for pupils, staring right at my door.

Nonono.

She took a step forward.

I ran over to my desk. Grabbed my cell phone. Started dialing 911. "Come on, come on..."

"911, what's your emergency?"

"I'm at the Greenbriar Motel and there's this guy, and this weird woman—"

Thump.

I was cut off by a loud thump nearby. I ran to the window and peered out.

The man who'd booked Room 7 was running towards the woman. He was holding something up in the air—a short dagger, gleaming silver in the rain. "He's attacking her!" I screamed into the phone.

The woman's face changed.

Her features twisted—her grin crept up to her eyes. Her arms crackled and stretched. She blinked, and her eyes turned pure white. Her body twisted unnaturally at the waist, so that she was facing the man.

With fast, jolted movements, she leapt at him.

Within seconds, he was dead. She stood on all fours above him, her knees bent the wrong way, her fingers far too long. With another horrible crackling sound, her neck stretched out two feet long, twisting and serpentine.

And then she looked at me.

I leapt away from the window with a scream. "What's happening?" the operator asked me. "Sir, please, tell me what's happening."

I opened my mouth. Tried to speak. But only a squeaking sound came out.

By the time I made it back over to the window, the

woman was standing there, looking down at her kill. She looked normal. Then she stepped over his body and walked towards the rooms.

To my horror, she pulled out a key and opened room 22.

Then she disappeared inside.

The police arrived a few minutes later. In strings of gibberish, I begged them to check room 22. That something horrible was lurking inside. But then they knocked on the door, a completely normal looking woman opened it.

I watched from the lobby. I couldn't hear that much of their conversation over the pouring rain, but they weren't arresting her. Weren't accusing her. They seemed to just be having a friendly conversation, asking her what she'd seen.

Then they thanked her and came back to me.

"We'll need to see the security tapes from tonight, please," the officer said, in an accusing tone.

But when I showed them the tapes, they got quiet. One of the officers made a call to someone, saying something about an "infestation." The other two officers ushered me out into the lobby, their faces grim. They told me not to leave as they talked among themselves in hushed voices in the corner of the room.

Then they approached.

"You didn't see anything tonight," the tall man said, leaning in close. "You got that?"

"I—but what about—"

"Listen to me very carefully," he interrupted,

lowering his voice. "You... didn't... see... anything. Just like you never shoplifted in your life."

"... What?"

"You understand me?" he asked.

The silence stretched out between us. "Yeah, I got it," I said, my voice wavering. "I didn't see anything."

I left the motel and never went back.

I planned to never speak of what I saw. To keep my mouth shut, just like they told me to. But after losing many nights of sleep, I realized that I need to warn people. I need to warn you. I can't have another person dying because of these *things,* whatever they are.

So, I beg you.

If you're driving through Michigan and see that there's a vacancy at the Greenbriar Motel—

Keep driving.

CHORES

My husband was first.

When I came home from work, I found my husband in the kitchen. Dishrag in hand, wiping down the counters. "Hi, babe!" he said, giving me a kiss.

Then he went right back to wiping.

Look. I love my family. They're wonderful. But 99% of the time, when I get home from work, the kids are on the TV and my husband is on his iPad.

"Thanks for cleaning," I said uneasily.

And then that little thought wormed its way into my head. *He's cleaning because he expects something in return.* Well, that was fine by me. I was tired, but I'd happily trade sexytimes for a clean kitchen.

But things got weirder when I walked into the living room.

My two kids weren't parked in front of the TV,

watching YouTube videos of toys being unboxed and cars crashing violently. Layla was putting her stuffies in a toy bin, and Ben was actually doing his homework.

I stood there in shock, staring at them.

"Hi Mommy!" Layla said, with a big smile. "Did you have a good day?"

Nonono. My daughter, who's usually using the sofa as a jungle gym and scribbling on the walls. She was asking me... if I had a good day?

"Uh, it was fine. Why's it so clean in here? Did Daddy take you out to the park for the day?"

She shook her head. "We've been drawing and stuff." She reached over to the pile of paper and pulled out a drawing. It depicted, in crude stick figures, me holding her hand. "I drew this for you, Mommy!"

I grabbed the drawing. It said I LOVE U MOMMY with a smiley face across the top. "Thanks... that's very sweet of you, Layla."

Things only got weirder from there. Dinner time is always a fight—my kids are picky as hell and someone always spits out food at some point. But Layla and Ben ate their dinners like two normal kids, without complaint. And then after—my husband started doing the dishes. *Without being asked.*

Cue Twilight Zone music.

This was getting too weird. Had they joined a cult? Watched some YouTube video about kindness and discipline? Was it another fake social media holiday like "daughters' day" or "sons' day," but honoring mothers? Or, was it just a good day? Occasionally, my kids were this well behaved. It was just the confluence of their behavior, *and* my husband's, that was super strange.

Around 7pm, my husband offered to watch the kids while I took a shower. But when I got out, I heard them talking in the family room. In low, hushed voices. I didn't even know my kids *could* talk at that volume.

I started for them—but I stopped in my tracks when I heard them say my name.

My name. Layla called me "Kate." Not "Mommy."

My blood turned to ice. I stood there, frozen, just beyond the doorway.

"I gave Kate my drawing," Layla said, with vocabulary and diction that seemed far too mature for a seven-year-old. "She seemed to like it."

"I did all my homework and cleaned the bathroom," Ben added. "It's spotless in there."

"Okay. Good job, both of you. We need to keep this up, okay? This is what husbands and children do."

With that, I heard footsteps coming my way. Heart hammering in my chest, I darted back for the stairs. As they came around the corner, I pretended I'd just come down. "You guys doing okay?" I asked, though my voice shook.

What the hell is going on here?

Layla ran up to me and grabbed my hand. My heart dropped at her ice-cold touch. "I want a bedtime story, Mommy!" she singsonged—her voice a completely different intonation than before.

"I want a bedtime story too!"

I glanced up at my husband. He shot me a warm smile. "Uh, could you put them to bed tonight? I'm not feeling great."

"Sure, honey!"

I listened to their footsteps, pounding up the stairs.

Then I got the fuck out of there.

I ran out to the car. Sat there for a moment, my entire body shaking. *Where are my babies?* Suddenly my heart ached for Layla's tantrums. For Ben's ear splitting shrieks as he played Minecraft. For the messes and spills and chaos.

Tears running down my cheeks, I started the car and began to back out of the driveway.

Beep, beep, beep.

The rear collision alert. I stomped on the brakes and glanced in the rearview mirror.

No.

My husband, Layla, and Ben were standing motionless in the darkness. Blocking my way out. They were no longer smiling.

Their faces were set in stone as they stared me down, scowling at me in the mirror. And their eyes... oh God, their eyes...

They were pure black.

Instinct shut in. I flipped the car into drive and pulled over the grass. Then I peeled out of the neighborhood.

It's been an hour now. I called the police, but they don't believe me. I don't know what to do next. My family... isn't acting like my family. I'm terrified. And more than anything, I miss my babies and my husband.

The good and the bad.

ALWAYS CHECK FOR YOUR SHADOW

Mom taught us one rule: *always check for your shadow.*

Every few hours, the three of us—Mom, Curlie, and me—would do a shadow check. It was as second nature as taking a sip of water. "Shadow check!" my mom would call, and we'd both look down, checking that our shadow was still there.

I thought everyone did this. We were homeschooled, so no one really told me otherwise. And my one friend down the block, Samantha, was a little strange herself, so she never seemed to notice.

But then Mom got a job, and Curlie and I went to school.

And that's when everything collapsed.

"What are you doing?" Paige asked me, as we stood outside for recess one cool fall afternoon.

"Shadow check," I replied, "*duh*."

"Shadow check?" she asked, confused. "What's that?"

I squinted at her. "You don't know what a *shadow check* is?"

It was like she'd told me she didn't know how to brush her teeth. I explained, slowly in simple terms, like I was talking to a baby: "You look at the ground. To check your shadow is still there."

She obediently looked at the ground. "There it is!"

Then she raised her arms out in front of her and linked them, making her shadow look like the letter P. "Look! It's like P, for Paige!"

In no time at all, half of the class was doing it. We'd bound out for recess, and someone would shout: "*Shadow check!*" The kids would contort their bodies into weird shapes to make their shadows look like elephants or cats or letters, and we'd try to guess what they were.

That went on nicely for about three days.

Then, horror struck.

On Thursday afternoon, it was overcast. "Shadow check!" Thomas shouted. I diligently looked down and saw my shadow.

But when I looked up, I realized—

Nobody else had a shadow.

For a second I wanted to panic. And scream. And run. But then I took a deep breath, and did exactly what my mom taught me.

I grabbed Paige first. "Hey!" she protested. But I didn't listen. I held on with a vice grip and started pulling her back towards the school. *When the shadow goes away, hide in darkness for a day.* The mantra echoed in my head. The school had a basement—I'd heard the teachers mention it. The basement would be safe. All we had to do was stay there until the morning.

"Let *go* of me!" Paige screeched, finally yanking her wrist out of my grasp. "What's *wrong* with you?!"

"What's wrong with *you?!*" I screamed back. "We have to hide!"

The kids weren't smiling anymore—they were staring at me, backing away, like I was a rabid animal.

"We have to hide!" I screamed again. "All the shadows are gone!" I grabbed at Paige again, but she dodged this time. I lost my footing and fell onto the asphalt. Pain stung my knees. I looked up at my classmates. *Why aren't they hiding?!*

"What are you doing?! *RUN!*" I screamed.

That's when a teacher helped me up—and took me right to the principal's office.

"I should have explained more clearly," my mother told that night, as she tucked me in. "The shadow thing is only for us. It's okay if other people don't have shadows."

"Why?"

Sadness flashed across her face for a second. Then she shook her head. "That's just the way it is."

No one talked to me at recess anymore. Not even Paige. I sat alone all the time. I noticed, now, that there were many days—and some classrooms, even—

when people didn't have shadows. I always did. But they didn't.

Months passed and eventually kids forgot about the incident. That's what kids do—forget. Sometimes I wish forgiving and forgetting came easier to adults. Paige would run up to me at recess and we'd play hopscotch. She never brought up the fact that even on an overcast day, my shadow still danced across the chalk lines, mirroring my own movements. Except sometimes, they were the slightest bit out of sync. Like my shadow was moving on a split second delay.

As I got older, however, things got more complicated.

In 7th grade science, the teacher taught us about the sun, and optics, and light. Prisms and rainbows and the cones and rods in our eyes. And she mentioned that our shadow was just the absence of light, that our bodies were blocking out the sun or the overhead fluorescent lights.

It didn't make sense to me, then, that my shadow —or anyone else's—would be able to disappear. If the lighting didn't change, and I didn't move... how could a shadow suddenly *disappear?*

Curlie was now old enough to insist we called her by her real name, but she was still too young to understand the argument I had with my mom that night. "It's not possible!" I shouted, as she worked on her coloring book upstairs. "You're *lying* to me!"

"I'm not lying to you," my mother pleaded.

"Yes, you are!"

I ran across the living room to get in my mom's

face. Walked right past the ornate glass lamp that stood on the end table.

My mom's eyes widened.

She looked at the ground.

And that's when I realized my shadow was gone.

The lamp was behind me. My shadow should have been on the floor in front of me. *But it wasn't.*

"Run," she whispered.

When I didn't move, she began to shout.

"Go to Curlie! GO!"

I hesitated for half a second. Then I sprinted for the stairs.

"TURN OFF THE LIGHT!" she shouted after me. I darted in and closed to the door. Then I bent down and yanked out the plug to the lamp. "Hey!" Curlie said. "I'm *coloring!*"

"Ssssh," I whispered.

"What—"

"My shadow disappeared."

Curlie was too young to remember the day her shadow disappeared. She'd only been a year old. Mom had scooped her out of the playpen, grabbed me by the hand, and took the three of us into the basement. We spent the night down there, in total darkness. Eating canned beans and sleeping on old comforters, laid out on the cement floor.

But she knew that it was bad. She scrambled over to her bed and pulled the covers over her head.

I stood in the center of the room, listening for Mom's footsteps.

They never came.

Is she staying down there?

But we had so many lights on down there. It would be safer to just run to us. I crept towards the door, my heart pounding, slipping over the Barbies Curlie had all over the floor. "Mom?" I called out, through the door.

Nothing.

I opened the door just a crack and peered out.

I could see the stairs, the light spilling out from the living room. But everything was silent. *Maybe she went into the basement. Maybe—*

A shadow appeared, cast across the wall.

No! She's still down there?!

But no. That couldn't be my mom's shadow. It was too short. And even though the edges were blurry, the shadow sort of looked like it had a ponytail. Not a short hair in a pixie cut, like my mom.

That's not mom.

That's me.

The blurry edges sharpened. And then the figure—the shadow—came into view. My ponytail, my upturned nose, my knock knees. The thing crouched down and pulled at something. Yanking it. Moving completely independent of me.

A dragging sound—

My mother's feet came into view.

Still and lifeless.

I gasped. My hand clapped to my mouth—but it was too late. The shadow froze.

Turned to stare directly at me.

And then with huge, loping strides, it started up the stairs—

I slammed the door shut. Clicked the lock. Then I jumped under the covers with Curlie, my entire body trembling.

The police never found Mom's body. She was eventually declared legally dead. Curlie and I were sent away to live with our grandparents. They didn't seem to know anything about the shadow—they never asked us to do shadow checks. The only remark in ten years was my grandma, on a particularly cloudy day, remarking how strange it was that I cast a perfect shadow on the sidewalk in front of us.

I watched it as I walked, and noticed its movements weren't perfectly in sync with my own.

As the years went by, and my shadow didn't disappear again, I started to get complacent. I checked for it less and less frequently. I started to lead a normal life, getting hired as a real estate agent. Curlie, now going by her name Rebecca, is nineteen and in college.

I even started to persuade myself that my shadow didn't kill her. That my mom ran away after our fight, and my memory of the shadow was my way of coping with it. Because it was harder to accept my mom had abandoned us than it was to accept an evil shadow had killed her.

That's what I told myself—until tonight.

As I sat down on my computer to finish writing a house listing, I noticed there was no shadow of my fingers on the keyboard.

No shadow on the linoleum under the desk.

I ran to turn off all the lights. But I don't think I was fast enough. Because when I ran to close the blinds, to block out the light from the streetlamp below—

I saw my shadow.

Walking across the dark street.

Disappearing into the night.

So please, I beg you. If you see any strange shadows in your home, or outside—something you don't think is cast by the lights, by the objects in your home—something that looks *different*—

Hide.

Somewhere pitch dark, where no shadows can be cast, until morning.

BE CAREFUL WHAT YOUR KIDS WATCH ON YOUTUBE

My kids watch a lot of YouTube. I'm not afraid to admit it. Sometimes I need a break. Sometimes I need to cook dinner. Sometimes I want to hide in the closet for fifteen minutes and cry my eyes out.

You know how it is as a parent.

Anyway. A few days ago, I put my kids on YouTube and walked away for a bit. I don't want to name specific names to incite a lawsuit here, but let's just say it's a very popular channel that follows the lives of several 3D-animated toddlers and their families. Let's call it BoBoPumpkin, but anyone who has kids knows exactly what channel I'm talking about.

Anyway. I put the TV on and walked away.

As I prepared dinner, however, I heard some strange audio coming from the TV. It sounded like the *Wheels on the Bus* song... the specific version from BoBoPumpkin I'd heard dozens of times... except weirdly distorted. Like it was being played back at half speed.

The wheels on the bus go rooooouuund and rooooouuund...

I left a half-chopped onion on the counter and walked into the living room. But when I saw the TV, I was shocked.

Some cheap rip-off channel, with a name in a language I didn't recognize, had stolen the audio and video for the classic BoBoPumpkin *Wheels on the Bus* song. Except—presumably, to avoid getting caught by YouTube's copyright filters—they'd changed it up. They'd changed the audio to half-speed or similar, making the voices low and distorted, almost demonic. They'd messed with the video multiple ways: turned it upside-down, switched up the colors (the bus was pink, the kid's skin was cyan blue), made two mirror images of it that intersected in the middle. These changes didn't happen all at once, but sequentially—a few seconds of upside-down, then a few seconds of weird colors... etc.

When I finally got over my shock, I immediately grabbed the remote and flipped it off. The kids didn't seem to care one way or the other, but I was thoroughly creeped out.

A few days passed. I kept a closer eye on the kids while they watched YouTube, but the video didn't come up again. I assumed that was the end of it.

I was wrong.

On Tuesday, after putting dinner on the table, I

called to the kids. "Johnny! Amelia!" I called. "Dinner's ready!"

No response.

Ugh. These kids never listen to me.

"Johnny! Amelia! Where are you?!"

Silence.

I charged up the stairs, ready to yell at them for not replying to me. But when I poked my head into Johnny's bedroom, he wasn't there. Amelia wasn't in her bedroom either.

My heart began to pound. "Johnny? Amelia?"

But then I heard it.

The horn on the bus goes beeeeep beeeeep beeeeep...

That distorted, half-speed audio from the video. Coming from my bedroom.

I burst into my room. And sure enough, I found them both sitting on my bed. Watching that cursed video on my TV.

"Johnny! Amelia!"

They didn't move.

They just stared at the screen, eyes glassy, bright colors flashing over their faces. Almost like they were hypnotized.

I grabbed the remote and turned the TV off. They slowly turned towards me. Sleepy, almost. Like they were just waking up.

"Didn't you guys hear me?" I asked.

Amelia shook her head. Johnny just stared.

"Come on. Dinner's ready."

But as we sat down to eat, a horrible feeling grew in the pit of my stomach.

That night, after the kids went to sleep, I uninstalled the YouTube app from both TVs. There was plenty to watch on Disney+, and there was even that new BoBoPumpkin show on Netflix. They'd have to just live without it for a while.

After cleaning up downstairs and locking up, I took a bath. I sunk into the warm water, taking deep breaths, entering relaxation mode. But only ten minutes later, I heard something coming from the other side of the door.

Music.

I strained my ears, listening.

It was muffled enough that I couldn't make out the singing. But from the pitch, I knew exactly what it was.

I got out of the tub. Wrapped a towel around myself. Burst into the bedroom.

The horn on the bus goes beeeeep beeeeep beeeeep...

I ran over to my phone, charging on the nightstand. Sure enough—it had YouTube open and was playing the video. I stared in horror as the blue-skinned bus driver slapped his hand on the horn. *Beeeeep. Beeeeep. Beeeeep.*

I grabbed the phone and turned it off.

It must've went off by accident.

Emerald must've tapped the phone, and they've been watching that video so much, it was probably right on my feed...

Our cat Emerald wasn't in my room now. But the

door was ajar. She could've gotten in, played with my phone, and accidentally opened YouTube. *Right?*

It was really unlikely. But I told myself those lies anyway. I couldn't go down that path, spiral into fear. I'd done it too many times as a single mom. Heard a noise in the middle of the night. Found a stray footprint in the yard. Saw someone I didn't recognize walking down the street, glancing at my house. Freaking out every time.

I was not going to lose my shit over some BoBoPumpkin video, of all things.

I dried off, got into my pajamas, and checked the kids. Then I turned off my phone, put on Airplane Mode so it didn't even have internet access, and went to sleep.

I woke up in the middle of the night.

I grabbed my phone off the nightstand and glanced at the time. 3:17 AM. I got up and used the bathroom. Then I decided to take a quick look at the kids—I'd check on them sometimes just to make sure everything was okay.

As soon as I got into the hallway, though, I saw something was terribly wrong.

Both of their doors were open.

My heart began to pound. "Johnny? Amelia?"

I ran to their rooms. Their beds were empty.

Oh no. No, no, no.

I ran down the stairs. *"Johnny! Amelia!"* I screamed. They didn't answer me—but I also didn't see any evidence of a break-in, a kidnapping, anything.

"WHERE ARE YOU?!"

As I made it to the foyer, I froze.

The basement door was ajar. And in the darkness, on the walls of the stairwell, I could see flickering blue light.

What the hell?

Our basement wasn't finished. But we did have a few things down there: an old sofa. Some boxes of toys. An old TV with an N64 and Super Nintendo that we sometimes played. Johnny and Amelia liked to play down there.

Maybe they got up in the middle of the night... couldn't sleep... and went down there to play?

I opened the door and stepped down onto the first step. The wood creaked underneath me. "Johnny? Amelia?" I called.

Nothing.

My heart pounded. I felt weak. Sick. I charged down the stairs, my hand slipping over the banister.

Halfway down, I heard it.

The daddies on the bus go 'I loooooove yoooooooou'...

That distorted, half-speed audio from the video.

I ran down the stairs.

Johnny and Amelia were sitting there. On the cold floor. In front of the old TV.

It was playing the video.

What the fuck? The TV down here was only connected to cable. It had no way of connecting to the internet. No way of getting to YouTube.

"Johnny! Amelia!"

They didn't move.

I watched in horror as the upside-down Daddy gave his son a hug. And then the video flipped back up, and their skin turned bluish-green. *'I loooooove yooooooou,'* said the warped, distorted audio. Static rippled across the image.

Johnny and Amelia stared at the TV, barely moving. The bright colors reflecting in their eyes. Their mouths hanging open. Hypnotized.

I ran over to the plug and yanked it out of the outlet. The TV flickered off with a staticky *whump* sound.

They slowly turned towards me.

"You're not supposed to be down here! It's the middle of the night!" I shouted.

"Sorry, Mommy," Amelia said.

"Why? Why do you want to watch this stupid video?!"

They didn't say anything.

"How did you even get it to play on here?"

Amelia got up. Then Johnny. Without a word, the two of them started up the stairs. I flicked off the lights and ran up after them.

I put them back to bed. Then I went back to my bedroom and tried to fall back asleep.

But I couldn't.

There must be some sort of hidden message in the video. Some sort of weird, covert hypnosis. Something to make the kids keep replaying it.

I'd read articles that the actual BoBoPumpkin channel itself was addictive and overstimulating, with its earworm songs and bright colors. Maybe this corrupted version was like that but on overdrive. Or maybe it was some hidden whispering or images that imprinted on the viewer's subconscious.

I grabbed my phone, opened YouTube, and played the video.

I studied it, staring at the grainy compression artifacts, the switched colors, the smiling 3D family with their oversized heads and perfect smiles. But there didn't seem to be any sort of horrible images or audio added. The song had been slowed down, and the video had been edited to be upside down, color swapped, all kinds of things like that... but nothing stuck out as sinister.

After five watches, I turned the phone off and went to sleep.

I hoped that would be the end of it.

I was wrong.

In the morning, while the kids were still sleeping, I unplugged all the TVs. I crept down the hall past their closed doors and headed downstairs, completely disconnecting the TV in the living room. And then the basement. They couldn't watch that stupid video anymore.

But unfortunately, the damage had already been done.

I heated up their breakfast and called for them. "Johnny! Amelia!"

They didn't come downstairs.

Calling them down from bed only worked about half the time under normal circumstances—and they were probably super tired this morning. I started up the stairs, to wake them up for school.

But when I opened their doors, my heart dropped through the floor.

Amelia was lying there in bed. But she wasn't asleep. Her eyes were open. She was staring straight up at the ceiling. Her pupils jittering back and forth.

As if she were *watching* something.

"Amelia!" I screamed. I grabbed her shoulders, gently shook her. "Amelia!"

Nothing.

When I burst into Johnny's room, it was the same thing. He was lying there on his side, with his eyes open. Staring straight at the wall. His pupils moving slightly back and forth, as if he were watching something projected on the blank wall.

"Johnny!"

It's been five hours now. I took them to the ER. The doctors have no idea what's wrong with them. They haven't spoken. They've barely even blinked. They've just been staring straight ahead, eyes jittering as if they're watching some invisible video I can't see.

And just a few minutes ago—for the first time today—Amelia made a noise, as she lay on the hospital bed next to her brother.

She was humming.

A slowed-down version of *Wheels on the Bus*.

THE STRANGE GROCERY STORE

I saw the job listing two weeks ago.

WANTED: NIGHT GUARD AT WESS MARKET IN [REDACTED], PA. 12AM-6AM SHIFT. $21/HOUR. The whole thing struck me as odd, right off the bat. What kind of grocery store needed a security guard while it was closed? Was the crime really that bad?

But I needed the money. Badly. And two days later, after a phone interview with a man named Clive, I showed up for my first shift.

As soon as I pulled up, I sort of understood why they needed a night guard. The grocery store sat at the edge of a run-down strip mall. Large signs reading SPACE FOR RENT hung in the store windows, but judging by the dusty glass and flickering streetlamps, no one had taken them up on the offer in years.

I parked near the front door. And as I approached the building, I saw a woman hurrying away from the store.

"You must be Aaron," she said breathlessly. "The night guard?"

"That's me."

"Clive left you some instructions. I put them on the conveyor belt at register 1." She gave me a polite nod and then stepped around me, heading for the only other car in the parking lot.

"Oh, thanks." *Be friendly,* my inner voice scolded. *She's your new coworker!* I turned around. "Hey, what's your name?"

But she was already diving into the car. The door slammed, the car reeled out of the parking space, and then she was gone.

So much for a new friend.

I turned back towards the store.

The parking lot was completely empty now, and the nearest streetlight was flickering with an odd, erratic rhythm. A cold wind swept in, whipping a crumpled paper bag across the parking lot.

Well, here goes nothing.

I stepped up to the store. The glass doors squeaked as they parted for me, and then I stepped inside.

Despite its outward appearance, the store was actually pretty nice inside. Bright fluorescent lights shone from overhead. Jazzy music played from hidden speakers. I headed over to register 1, where a folded piece of paper was waiting for me.

I flipped it open and began to read.

Dear Aaron,

Welcome to the Wess family! We sincerely

hope you enjoy your first shift. To help you, we've compiled a list of rules that should make your shift as easy as our fresh-baked apple pie.

1. As night guard, you are expected to patrol the store every half hour, making sure nothing is amiss. You may spend the rest of your time in the break room, at the back of the store, monitoring the security camera feeds.
2. Do not go down aisle 7. Do not look down aisle 7.
3. If you hear a knocking sound coming from within the freezers in the frozen food aisle, ignore it.
4. If you see a shopping cart that hasn't been put away, please return it to the shopping carts at the front of the store immediately.
5. Do not be alarmed if you find a pool of blood in the meat aisle. Sometimes our meat packages leak. Simply head to the storage closet, get the mop and bucket, and clean it up. However, do not step in the puddle or touch it in any way.
6. If you see a woman in the store, immediately go to the break room and stay there until she leaves. Do not call the police or report a break in. Do not make eye contact with her.

7. **The music we play throughout the store is a prerecorded disk of instrumental jazz. If the music ever stops, immediately go to the break room and stay there until it resumes.**
8. **Do not, under any circumstances, end your shift early.**

Thank you so much and again, I hope you enjoy your shift!

- **Clive**

I stared at the rules, re-reading them slowly. They were so weird. A woman in the store? Avoid aisle 7? I'd never been given instructions like this, even when I worked as a bouncer at a nightclub in a bad part of town.

Maybe it was a test. They wanted to see how well I could follow instructions, no matter how absurd they were. I looked up at the security camera, staring down at me from the corner.

Okay. Challenge accepted.

I glanced at my phone. 12:06. *Might as well get my first patrol out of the way now, before getting settled in.*

It was odd walking through the store when it was so empty and quiet. All the breads and muffins had been stored away somewhere. White opaque plastic had been pulled down over the vegetable display, to keep the cold in. When I got to the end, I made a right into the meat section.

Sheets of plastic had been pulled over the meat coolers, too. I saw flashes of red through the gaps, of massive ribeye and sirloin steaks, big slabs of meat with the bone still intact. I averted my eyes—while I wasn't a vegetarian, I never really liked the sight of raw meat. I turned instead to the aisles. Aisle 3: pasta and sauces, all lined up on the shelves, glinting in the fluorescent light. Aisle 4: cookies and snacks. Aisle 5, Aisle 6—

Oh right. I wasn't supposed to look at Aisle 7.

I forced myself to look down at the floor. Yeah, it was stupid, but they told me not to look. In the off chance they were going to check the CCTV footage later to grade my performance, I was going to follow every rule.

I continued further into the store. A few minutes later, I found the break room; a nondescript brown door with a little square window cut into it. I took note of its location for later—as soon as I was done with this patrol, I was going to break out my laptop and finish watching *Friday the 13th IV*.

And then I was at the west end of the store—the frozen section. I turned down the aisle, heading back towards the front.

That's when I saw it.

A shopping cart, parked askew in the middle of the aisle.

I huffed. Of all the rules, this was the one that annoyed me the most. I was hired to be a security guard—not a cleanup crew. Wasn't it the employees' job to put all the carts away at closing time?

Sighing, I began pushing it towards the front of the store.

The wheels rolled smoothly underneath me. The jazz music played softly in my ears. I turned the corner and walked past the cash registers, heading towards the front door.

That's when I heard it.

A soft sound. Barely audible over the jazz music. I stopped, straining my ears to listen. Several seconds of silence went by; and then I heard it again.

It sounded like someone crying.

The hairs on my neck stood on end. *There's no one in here. The door's been locked the whole time.* Unless... unless a customer had accidentally stayed past closing time. Maybe that employee, the woman I'd run into in the parking lot, didn't notice them. And locked up before they could get out.

"Who's there?" I called out.

A wailing sob, in response.

My heart plummeted. It sounded like a woman, or possibly even a child. "I'm coming!" I called, breaking into a run. "Where are you?"

They didn't reply—they just kept sobbing. I frantically continued in the direction of the sound, calling out to them, telling them everything would be okay.

But then I stopped dead.

The sound... it was coming from Aisle 7.

Do not go down aisle 7. Do not look down aisle 7. The rules had been very clear about that. I stopped just short of the aisle, next to an endcap display of mayonnaise, and carefully positioned myself so I was hidden.

"I'm going to help you," I called out. "Can you tell me what happened?"

They finally spoke. But they didn't answer my question. "H-help me," the voice cried, through more sobs. "P-please."

I wanted to step into the aisle. My foot was already halfway off the floor, ready to run in there and comfort them. But something stopped me. A gut instinct, a little alarm bell going off in my head. Because out of all the aisles... what were the chances this person would be in Aisle 7?

And besides, they were safe. They were in an empty store with me. It's not like they were in a dark alleyway in the middle of the night.

"Come out of the aisle," I called, my voice shaking a little. "Then I'll be able to help you."

"Please," the voice replied. "Help me."

This is stupid. Clearly some person got stuck in here after closing time, and they're scared. Just go into the aisle and help them get home. But there was another part of my brain, the instinctual, lizard-brain part. And it was screaming at me to not move a muscle.

"Do you need me to call someone?" I tried. "Your parents or family? The police?"

"H-help me," the voice pleaded again.

The *help me*. It sounded the same, each time they said it. A little stutter at the beginning. An emphasis on *me*. It almost sounded like a recording, or some AI-generated thing, looping over and over. It didn't sound... natural.

"Come out of the aisle!" I shouted. "Come out, and I'll help you!"

The sobs got louder, faster. Hysterical. "Help me!" the voice pleaded again, in a desperate tone that made my stomach twist.

I stood there, pressed against the mayonnaise display. Listening to them sob was making my stomach flip-flop—even if it did sound slightly unnatural. *I could call the police*, I thought. They'd know what to do.

Except I'd left my cell phone with my backpack at cash register 1. And getting it would mean crossing Aisle 7.

The rules didn't say anything about walking past Aisle 7. They just said I shouldn't go down it or look down it. And I couldn't just stand here and do *nothing*. What if it really was someone who needed help? A child who'd sprained their ankle and couldn't get up?

"Don't worry. I'm getting my phone and calling the police," I called out. Then I took a deep breath and stepped across the threshold of Aisle 7, towards register 1.

As soon as I took a step, the crying stopped. Just like that. Violent sobbing and then—in an instant—nothing. Like a switch had flipped.

Then the footsteps started.

Loud, slapping footsteps of someone running down the aisle. Way too large to be a child. Coming straight at me. My heart dropped—*it's a trap, they're coming for me and I'm probably going to die here—*

But as soon as I made it across the aisle, the sound stopped. All I heard were the soft jazz tunes playing through the speakers overhead.

I hightailed it to the break room, completely forgetting about the cart I was supposed to return.

The break room was small and cramped. The little square window in the door had been blacked out with construction paper from the inside. The only source of light came from the computer screen on the desk, displaying the security camera feeds.

I scrolled through the feeds. I quickly noticed that none of them offered coverage of Aisle 7. It seemed like the cameras were intentionally placed to avoid that aisle. After searching the grainy black-and-white video for anything amiss, I leaned back in the chair and closed my eyes.

When I finally opened them again, it was almost 12:30.

Time for my next patrol.

I didn't want to go. I felt safe here, locked up in this little room. But I also knew I wouldn't be safe if I didn't listen to the rules. I shuddered, imagining what would've happened to me if I'd gone down Aisle 7. If I hadn't listened.

I pulled myself out of the seat and headed for the door.

The store was completely silent. No hysterical sobbing or pounding footsteps. I started my patrol near the back, walking up aisle 17. Cans of food glinted on the shelves as I passed; but when I glanced at them, I didn't see any labels I recognized. No chef ravioli or giant green men. Just generically labeled cans of meat stew.

In fact, all the aisle had was meat stew. The same cans, over and over and over.

I reached the end and turned right, towards the front of the store. And that's when I realized that I had, already, broken one of the rules.

The cart.

I hadn't returned it.

It wasn't where I'd left it—instead of haphazardly parked near aisle 7, it sat next to one of the cash registers. Like some ghost man was checking out his groceries. I paused for a second, hands hovering above the handle. Then I grabbed it and headed towards the door.

Outside, the parking lot was pitch black. Not a single streetlamp. *The shopping carts are only a few feet from the door*, I told myself. *Just go in and out. It'll take two seconds.*

I did it as quickly as possible. I ran into the darkness, slammed the shopping cart into the row, and dashed back inside. Then I shut the doors and clicked the lock. "Okay. That wasn't too bad," I said to myself, letting out a sigh of relief.

For a second, I reveled in the peace of the store.

The silence. The safety of being locked inside, with no one else with me.

But then I stopped.

The silence.

Oh, no.

The jazz music wasn't playing.

How long had it been off? I'd been so preoccupied with returning the cart, I wasn't even paying attention. I broke into a sprint towards the back of the store, cookies and snacks flashing by me. Then I swerved right and sprinted into the break room.

I pulled out the list of rules and read them over again. *Do not, under any circumstances, end your shift early.* Why did he write that? Was it just because he didn't want anyone flaking out on him? Or if I left early, would some horrible fate befall me?

Because I really, *really* wanted to leave.

I opened my backpack, pulled out the soda I'd brought, and popped it open. Took a sip. Scrolled through the security feed.

Five more hours.

The next four patrols went fairly well.

The rules didn't say how long they had to be. So every thirty minutes, I sprinted a lap around the store, as fast as I could. The whole thing only took about a minute. Then, for the other 29, I locked myself in the break room.

On the second patrol, I heard knocking as I ran

down the freezer aisle. It started as light tapping across the glass, then crescendoed into loud *thumps*, like someone was slamming their palms against the glass doors. As per the rules, I ignored it. I just kept running, until I made it back to the break room.

On the last patrol, the music had cut out again. So I quickly detoured and got to the break room as quickly as I could, the silence ringing in my ears.

And now, here I was in the break room, with three hours left.

I stared at my phone's clock, ticking slowly towards 3 AM. I stood up, shaking out my nervous energy, preparing myself to sprint. I'd been a runner back in high school, but in the past ten years I'd gotten way out of shape. The last patrol had left me panting and breathless, legs aching.

My hand closed around the doorknob. My heart hammered in my chest. *Three, two, one... go.* I wrenched the door open and shot out into the store.

But I didn't get very far.

Because there was an enormous pool of blood on the floor.

I froze. All the air sucked out of my lungs. I stared at the blood, shining in the fluorescent lights. *The rules said to clean it up.* But that would take at least ten minutes. I wasn't safe out here.

I swallowed.

Then I hurried to the supply closet. Got a mop and a bucket. And started cleaning as fast as I could.

The job was messy. I slid the mop through the blood, then dunked it in the bucket. Rinsed and repeated. The soapy water tinged red. A few times it splashed up and almost landed on me.

But I did it. I cleaned it all up without touching a drop. Unfortunately, by the time I was finished, it was 3:27. Time for my next patrol.

I was too tired to run, so I settled for a brisk walk around the store. I headed up through the frozen food. I noticed, now, there were handprints on the glass doors—handprints of all sizes, tilted and smudged. Except the proportions looked all wrong, with fingers that were too long, too thin. I averted my eyes and kept going.

Two and a half more hours.

My footsteps clicked against the tile floor. The jazz was starting to grate on my nerves—I must've heard the same, looping saxophone melody twenty times now. It made me want to punch something. Sighing, I continued towards the produce section, briskly walking past the aisles.

Then I stopped.

Something caught my eye, in one of the aisles. I backed up and took a better look.

Someone was standing in Aisle 9.

A woman. She wore a blue linen dress and black high heels. Long, black hair cascaded down her back, almost to her waist. She faced away from me, standing still, her thin white arms hanging limply at her sides. In her hand was a basket, filled with cuts of raw meat.

The rule echoed in my head. *If you see a woman in*

the store, immediately go to the break room. Do not make eye contact with her.*

I slowly backed up, as quietly as I possibly could. Then I started down the next aisle, towards the break room.

Click, click, click.

I heard her footsteps echo against the tile. I hurried my pace towards the break room—but then I stopped. Her footsteps weren't coming from behind me. They were coming from in front of me.

I averted my eyes to the floor—just as I saw two black, high-heeled shoes step into the aisle.

I stared at the floor. *Do not make eye contact with her. Do not make eye contact with her.* The words repeated over and over in my head. But I had to get to the break room—and she was standing in my way.

All I could see were her shiny, high-heeled shoes. And the little drops of blood that leaked out of the meat packages in her basket, staining the floor.

I backed up. That was the only way I *could* go. I kept my eyes on the floor, careful not to look up. But she was following me. *Click, click.* For every step I took, I saw a shiny black heel come into view, attached to a thin, white calf extend. Keeping time with me.

I quickened my pace. So did she.

Click-click-click.

I wheeled around and broke into a sprint.

Clickclickclick—

I ran down an aisle at random and sprinted

towards the break room. But then, halfway down the aisle, I stopped.

A shopping cart was parked across the middle of the aisle, blocking my way.

Not just one cart. Several of them, stacked up in a teetering tower that was nearly as tall as the aisles themselves.

I was trapped.

I backed away, my heart pounding.

Click.

Slow, methodical footsteps. Coming towards me, slowly, like a cat stalking its prey.

I took my chances. I turned around, sprinted back out into the open, and stepped into the next aisle—

Oh, no, no.

I knew it instantly. A tattered lump of gray clothing and sickly, pale-blue skin sat on the floor. The person—the creature—the *thing* folded in on itself, in a pose reminiscent of a crying child. But it obviously wasn't anything resembling a human, with its strange lumps and appendages and complete lack of head.

I'd stepped into Aisle 7.

I immediately reversed direction. But not before the *thing* unfolded itself and began to move towards me. I whipped around and, screaming, sprinted down the next aisle.

Miraculously, I made it to the end in one piece. I veered sharply left, towards the break room. *Almost there... almost there.*

My hand hit the doorknob. I wrenched it open and dove inside. Then I collapsed in the chair, panting.

I sucked in a breath, staring at the locked door. *Am I really safe in here?* Technically, the rules never said I would be safe. Maybe staying in here only decreased my chance of death.

I turned my attention to the security camera feed on the monitor. It showed the middle of the store, and from what I could see, the aisles were empty—no trace of the woman. I switched to the next feed. The produce section. Empty. I switched to the next one—

I jumped.

She was standing *right there.*

In front of the break room door.

She stood so still, the image could've been a photograph—except for the blood slowly dripping from the meat in her basket. I swallowed and glanced away from the monitor, at the door. My heart slammed into my ribs when I saw her shadow under the door.

Go away. Please, go away, I pleaded in my mind.

The shadow of her head in the window tilted, as if contemplating her next move. Now I knew why the window had been covered.

I forced my eyes away and looked back at the screen.

She was still standing there. Except, there was something... *different* about the way she was standing. I squinted at the grainy black and white image, trying to figure out what was going on. When my eyes finally fell on her heels, I realized.

They were facing forward.

But I was still looking at the back of her head. At the long, black hair cascading to her waist.

Either her hair was hanging over her face... or she'd turned her head all the way around.

It must've been twenty minutes before she began to walk away from the door. I couldn't tell if it was just the low framerate of these crummy cameras, but her movements looked jerky, her body lurching with each step.

It made me sick to watch.

When she disappeared from the screen, I let out a breath of relief. My hands and legs were shaking, weak. *Okay. Think.* The rules said to wait until she left. All I had to do was watch the feed by the front door. As soon as I saw her leave the store, I'd be safe.

After a few minutes of sitting there, waiting for my heart rate to return to normal, I forced my fingers back to the keyboard. I pressed the arrow key, to move to the next feed. Then the next, and the next, looking for the camera at the front of the store—

No.

Her face. Her face filled the entire screen.

Her eyes filled me with horror. They were pure white—no pupils, no irises, just pure white eyes threaded with spidery veins.

I screamed and jumped back. Then I shut my eyes. *The rules said don't make eye contact!* Did that count? Through the screen? I let out a terrified, shuddering wail and covered my face with my hands, my entire body shaking.

When I finally took a peek through my fingers, I saw her. Rapidly scaling down the wall, away from the camera on the ceiling, like some kind of spider. Then she pushed through the glass doors and disappeared into the night.

She'd left.

I was safe. Or as safe as I could be, in this cursed grocery store. I glanced at the clock. 3:58 AM. Time to patrol.

I really didn't want to. But I forced myself to swing the door open and run as fast as I could through the store. I saw shopping carts stacked in teetering towers. Heard hands pounding against the freezer doors. Saw little spots of blood on the shiny tile, from the woman as she'd stalked me.

And then, a minute later, I was done. I locked myself in the break room, and for the first time in years, began to sob.

The remaining patrols went by without incident —though I did hear more sobbing from Aisle 7 and more banging from the freezers. And then, the hour had come. 6 AM. My heart soared at the sight of the pink dawn sky through the glass doors. I was safe. I was free.

When I glanced out into the parking lot, I saw a few cars pulling in. Disgruntled, groggy employees clutching coffees, heading towards me. As soon as the first one came in, I flew out of the store, ran to my car, and got out of there as fast as I could.

I'd never felt such relief. Such happiness. I felt like a new man. All of my problems, even my financial ones, seemed dwarfed by what I'd just endured. When I pulled onto the main road, I rolled down my windows and flicked on the radio.

But it wasn't my usual classic rock station that blared through the speakers.

Instead, I heard the upbeat tune of a saxophone.

And as I listened to that horrible, looping melody, I realized that my days as a night guard for Wess Market may not be over yet.

THERE'S SOMETHING WRONG WITH THE MOON

There's something wrong with the moon.

I first noticed it as I was driving home from work. Through the crisscrossing branches of the treetops, I saw a flash of white. And my brain immediately thought it was some sort of early Christmas decoration, like a lit star, on top of a building.

Of course, a second later, I realized it was the moon. But I could see why my brain went there: it looked just a little bigger, a little brighter, than it should've been. A big white ball, shining down on me like an eye.

Throughout the drive home, as soon as the moon peeked into view, my eyes immediately snapped to it. It was jarring, different. As products of evolution, our brains are programmed to notice changes in our surroundings. New things. Different things. It's why we notice a speck of dirt on the floor, instead of the dozens of whorls in the wood or the way the carpet fibers push together. Our eyes go to it because it's different.

And my eyes kept going to the moon.

When I got home, I told my husband. "The moon looks weird."

He joined me at the window. We stared up at it together. It was perfectly full—a perfect circle floating in the endless expanse of space.

"Wait—wasn't it just a crescent moon a few days ago?" Rich asked me.

"Maybe..."

I pulled out my phone. I searched for a few minutes, and then I found it: a moon calendar. My heart dropped.

"It's supposed to be a new moon right now."

Rich took the phone from me and stared at it. "What?"

We both looked at the calendar. Then I searched for more moon calendars. But they all said the same thing: tonight was supposed to be a new moon.

I started through the house, closing the blinds. Rich followed me. "What are you doing?"

"I don't want to see it anymore!" I snapped.

He stepped back, surprised at my sudden anger. I didn't blame him. I, too, was surprised by how panicked my voice sounded. "What if it's some kind of spy weather balloon, or UFO, or something? That's designed to *look* like the moon, so no one questions it?"

"Then they did a shitty job. They should've looked

at the moon calendar before designing it, or sent it up when it was a full moon."

"Or maybe there are other factors at play. Maybe they can only send it up during certain weather conditions. So they had to send it up tonight."

I continued closing the curtains. Through the translucent, gauzy ones in the living room, I could still see it: a foggy, glowing sphere above the treetops. A chill ran down my spine.

I started upstairs. But when I walked over to the window, ready to close the curtains, I froze.

Thick clouds had rolled in. But they weren't in front of the moon—they were *behind* it.

"Rich!" I shouted. "Rich, *look!*"

I pointed at the sky, shaking. He stared up at it, confused; then his face dropped with realization. He reached up and pulled the curtains closed with a metallic *schling*.

We went back downstairs and turned on the local news. But there was nothing about it—nothing about the fake moon floating in the sky.

"It can't be that high up," I whispered, "if it's in front of the clouds."

"It's probably one of those spy balloons... like you said."

I texted a few of our friends in town. Only one texted back; he'd noticed the moon looked bright, but hadn't thought through it more than that. Now he was freaking out just like we were, as he noticed the clouds behind the "moon" just like we did.

As Rich and I sat together, talking about what this

could possibly be, something caught my eye.

Movement.

Through the translucent curtains in the living room.

I ran to the window. Parted them, slightly. I gasped as I watched the moon… ripple? That was the only way I could describe it. Like the image was some huge piece of cloth, balloon or otherwise, hit with a gust of wind. The craters rippled and shivered—

And then the moon went out.

As my eyes adjusted to the darkness, I could barely make out a black, circular silhouette floating up in the sky where the moon had been.

It floated upwards and disappeared.

This was about a week ago. Since nothing else happened, and the balloon or whatever it was didn't reappear, I thought that was the end of it. Whatever it was, it'd completed its journey and moved on to other things.

But I was wrong.

Because this morning, I received a text message from an unverified number.

It was a photo. An aerial view of our house, taken from maybe a thousand feet up. Detailed enough that I could make out the half-built garden in our backyard, the chairs on our deck. After talking to our friends, we learned they'd received similar images—of their own houses, in startling detail.

But we all got the same message.

Two words, below the image.

WE'RE WATCHING

MONSTER IN YOUR CLOSET

"There's a monster in my closet, Daddy!"

My daughter's voice, calling out into the hallway.

I lay down and closed my eyes, sleepiness washing over me. I listened to my husband, Rob, walk into her bedroom. "Kayla, there's nothing in your closet," I heard him say, muffled through the wall.

I smiled. He was such a good dad. No one like him in the world. Kayla was so lucky to have him. She was his whole world.

"There *is!* I saw it, I saw it!"

"Okay, okay. I'll go check for you."

I listened to Rob's footsteps thump across the carpet. Heard the doorknob turn, the door creak open.

And there he was. Standing over me.

I smiled up at him from the closet floor.

His eyes widened. He clamped a hand over his mouth. Then he slammed the door shut and ran back to the bed.

I heard him sobbing in Kayla's room. Heard her terrified voice. "Daddy, daddy, what's wrong? Did you see it, too?"

Deep sadness crushed me. All I wanted to do was spend time with Kayla. Read her a bedtime story, after she fell asleep.

I can't help it that I've been dead for two weeks.

That my skin is decomposing and melting off my face.

That worms poke holes in my cheeks and wind through my teeth.

When Rob found that spell book, to bring me back to life, I don't think he realized…

It would bring my soul back—

But it wouldn't restore my body.

HAS ANYONE HEARD OF THE BLOODWORTH INCIDENT?

It was only my second day when I first heard about the "Bloodworth incident." Janelle brought it up while we were eating lunch. "Of course, after the Bloodworth incident, my wife and I got an entire home security system. It cost a fortune, but it's worth the peace of mind."

I wasn't really interested in the conversation—I was more interested in scarfing down the burrito in front of me—so I didn't ask what the "Bloodworth incident" was.

But then it came up again. And again. And again...

Stan: "We haven't left our curtains open since Bloodworth."

Caitlyn: "I probably would've been a nurse forever, if Bloodworth had never happened. But I just didn't feel safe anymore."

Larry: "Did you catch that special on the Bloodworth Incident last night?"

Unlike my coworkers, I was new to Green Creek. I figured "the Bloodworth incident" was some sort of local thing that happened a few years ago. Maybe a convict escaped from prison named Bloodworth. Maybe there was an accident on Bloodworth Street, or a flu outbreak named "Bloodworth." I was curious, but the social pressure to appear like everyone else kept me from asking.

But then, the comments got weirder.

"I'm writing a novel for NaNoWriMo this year," Aaliyah said during lunch. "It's about what life would be like, if the Bloodworth incident had never happened."

"Ooooh, that's such a good idea!" Stan said.

"That sounds *so* interesting. I would *love* to read that," Janelle said.

Wait. What? Now they were talking about it like it was a national, life-altering disaster. Not just some local incident. There was a pause in the conversation, and I finally took my chance. "Wait, sorry, I'm confused. What's the 'Bloodworth incident'?"

Aaliyah looked me dead in the eye. And then—she burst into laughter. Slowly, my other coworkers broke into laughter, too. Until everyone at the table was chuckling.

"You're funny, Amanda," Aaliyah said, shooting me a grin. "I like you."

I wanted to say *no, I'm serious, what is it?* But there was something about the atmosphere that made me uncomfortable. So I said nothing.

When I got home, I spent an hour on Google.

Bloodworth Incident. Bloodworth Green Creek Pennsylvania. Nothing came up. I tried multiple combinations of keywords, even fiddling with the time range for search results, and still—nada.

But when I woke up the next morning, everything was crystal clear.

It's a prank. A sort of hazing ritual, for new hires. It made sense—the software development team was a rambunctious, loosey-goosey crowd. Stan swore all the time; Caitlyn came to work in sweatpants. Lunchtime conversation included borderline inappropriate topics, like past tales of drunken revelry or TMI details of Stan's recent divorce.

This is exactly the kind of thing they'd pull.

Besides, if "the Bloodworth incident" really happened... they wouldn't mention it *so* often. It came up almost every day! Like they were *trying* to talk about it as much as possible.

Unfortunately, I couldn't confront them today. It was a Saturday. So I spent my morning at the local coffee shop, getting some editing work done for my side hustle.

That's when things got weird.

Two young women sat down at the next booth, talking loudly about the party last night. And a few minutes into their conversation, I heard them mention it.

I haven't slept through the night since the Bloodworth incident.

I froze.

So it wasn't some prank in the office. It was something other people knew about in the town. For a minute, I just sat there in silence, my mind reeling. Then I cut in.

"Excuse me—sorry to bother you, but—could you tell me what the Bloodworth Incident is?"

Both of the girls turned to me. Then the brunette one stood up. "Uh, sorry, we have to go," she said quickly.

I watched as the two girls hurried out, glancing back to make sure I wasn't following.

I called my mom that afternoon. She had never heard of the Bloodworth Incident. I texted a few of my friends. They also had no idea what it was.

I drove to a Walmart just a few miles outside the town's border. Struck up a conversation with the cashier and mentioned the Bloodworth incident. She stared up at me with wide blue eyes. "The *what* incident?"

I drove back into town, on the narrow two-lane route that snaked through the forest. Just beyond the old, hand-painted *Welcome to Green Creek* sign, there was a little gas station. It looked like it'd seen better days, from the paint peeling on the mini-mart to the rust creeping up the sides of the pumps.

I went into the mini-mart, poured myself a coffee, and made my way to the bored-looking man sitting behind the counter.

"Coffee? This late?" he asked, with a smile. It was almost 7—starting to get dark.

"Haven't been sleeping much since Bloodsworth," I replied, pulling out my wallet.

A pause.

"Oh, yeah, it's been crazy. Sometimes I get up in the middle of the night and check the locks." He rang up my coffee. "Two-thirteen."

I handed him my card. And then I decided to push a little. "Aren't you afraid he might break in through the windows?"

He looked up at me, brows furrowed. "'He'?"

"Sorry, I meant... 'she'?"

His expression darkened. His gaze flicked to the door—and then he stood up, taking a step towards me. *What is he doing?* Every muscle in my body froze. *Is he going to... try something? Get out, get out now—*

"You don't know what the Bloodworth incident is, do you?" he asked.

"No..."

"You sure as hell better not let anyone know."

I stood there, frozen. Stunned. Seconds later, the bells jingled behind me as another customer entered. He smiled and waved. Like nothing had happened.

I turned on my heel and ran back to the car.

It was starting to get dark. Deep blue shadows stretched across the road from the bare trees, like giant claws. I started up the car and pulled out onto the road, headlights blaring into the darkness.

Don't let anyone know. Why? Was it some sort of conspiracy? Or a cult thing? Maybe a cult leader lived in town. Maybe he'd brainwashed everyone here, and invented an 'incident' to fearmonger his followers into behaving. Or, maybe *not* knowing about the incident was some sort of signal. That I wasn't a member of the cult. That I should be hunted down.

As I drove down Main Street, I passed the town library. But then an idea hit me. I made a U-Turn and pulled into the tiny parking lot.

A woman sat behind the desk, working a computer that looked like it was from two decades ago. She reminded me of a huggable little grandmother, with her oversized spectacles, gray hair, and knit sweater.

"Do you keep old newspapers? Like, local ones, from a few years ago?"

"Of course," she replied, with a sweet smile. "You can find them down there."

I walked down one of the aisles, to where the microfilms were kept. My footsteps sounded loud in the silence, echoing among the dusty books. I grabbed a film from 2000 and started my search, scanning article after article on the screen.

Looking for any mention of the *Bloodworth Incident*.

I honestly didn't expect to find anything. But then I came across an issue of *The Green Creek Sentinel* from July 3, 2005.

Heart hammering, I began to read.

TOWN ROCKED BY 'BLOODWORTH INCIDENT'
by JODIE McFARLANE

On the morning of July 2, a horror shook our little town of Green Creek, Pennsylvania. Nearly half of our residents woke to find their front doors mysteriously open, with a dark, sticky substance pooled on the floor.

But that was only the beginning. Those residents began to exhibit

CONTINUED ON PAGE 2

I flipped the page—and gasped.

The entire article was scribbled out with black marker. There was even a photo—a photo of the Main Street. Grainy, black and white. I could make out the library, the other shops, the sky... but the marker had scribbled over most of the street.

But not fully. I could make out a pair of shoes. As if someone were lying there. A body.

And if I used my imagination, based on how many scribbled-out blobs there were, I'd guess there were no less than twenty bodies in the middle of the street.

I clapped a hand to my mouth. I clicked wildly at the mouse, moving through the next few issues, looking for any mention of Bloodworth. I didn't find any.

But I did find something.

A TRIBUTE TO JODIE McFARLANE

We sadly mourn the death of our very own head journalist, Jodie McFarlane. She was only 41 years old...

A voice snapped me out of my trance.

"What are you doing?"

I whipped around.

The librarian was standing right behind me. But she didn't look so warm and fuzzy now. Her expression was dark, stone-like, as she stared at the screen in front of me. A quiet fury in her eyes, behind her glasses.

"I'm sorry... I was just—"

"You came here to find out about Bloodworth, didn't you?" she snarled.

"I—"

"You don't know about it. *You're one of them!*"

I expected her to lunge at me. Grab me. Chase me. But instead, she tilted her head towards the ceiling and let out the most blood-curdling scream I've ever heard.

Shuffling, rustling sounds echoed from the other aisles.

I broke into a run. Leapt past her, sprinting as fast as I possibly could. Once I made it to the atrium, I glanced back. Three other townspeople were running towards me, shouting to each other.

I ran for my life.

Miraculously, I made it out to the car. As I pulled away, I saw them standing at the door, staring at me.

Like an idiot, I thought I'd lost them. But as soon as I pulled out onto Main Street, I heard a police siren pierce the air. Red-and-blue lights flashed in my rearview.

I pushed the pedal to the floor.

As soon as I crossed the town's boundary—the gas station, the sign—the officer pulled off to the side of the road. He didn't follow me. He just watched me, as I sped away from that place.

I never went back. Never got my stuff. I got a new

job, moved three states away, and started my post-college life over again. I assumed that was the end of it, and I'd never hear about the Bloodworth Incident again.

I was wrong.

Several months after the move, I met someone. He just moved to my city, and our dates have been phenomenal. I've taken him to the best restaurants and museums, showed him everything there is to do here. We were just about to celebrate our first month together—when he said something that stopped me in my tracks.

"You really should get a deadbolt for the door," he said casually, as we watched TV on the couch. "'Cause, we wouldn't want another Bloodworth incident. Would we?"

STRANGE DOG

I live in a small town. We have a pet store that's owned by a local family. It has mice, snakes, ferrets, and various birds. We even have a few dogs and cats from the local animal shelter.

In general, I've enjoyed my job here. I've always loved working with animals. Of course we've had our fair share of problems—I still remember the time that Chihuahua bit me—but in general, I love it here.

That all changed with the arrival of Lucy.

Lucy was a mixed breed. We weren't really sure what breeds were in her heritage, but my coworker Andi and I had fun guessing. She had a fluffy undercoat and curled tail, which made me think husky, Malamute, or even Samoyed. Her ears were floppy though, and her fur was this sort of unique gray color, making Andi guess part Greyhound or Weimaraner. She also had blue eyes, which is quite rare.

There was no denying she was a beautiful dog.

But as soon as she arrived at the pet store, everything started going wrong.

I still remember the day I brought her into the dog room. At the time, we had a German Shepherd and a small mixed breed dog. As soon as we entered the room, both of them started growling at her. Teeth bared. Hackles raised. Staring at her.

I'd never seen them growl like that.

"Hey, it's okay," I said, trying to soothe them. The German Shepherd let out a guttural bark. The small dog retreated to the corner of his crate, trying to get as far away from her as possible. I led Lucy to her cage and shut the door, hoping the dogs would calm down.

They didn't.

Two hours later, the dogs were still growling and barking. And the strangest thing of all was that Lucy didn't seem bothered by it. She just lay there in her crate, looking at them calmly, perfectly still.

We eventually decided to move Lucy to the cat room. We weren't housing any cats at the time, and our manager said she'd reschedule the future cat adoptions for a week or two, until the dog was adopted. "Shouldn't take long, for a beautiful dog like that," she said.

"She's quiet, too. Barely barks or anything," I replied.

But a week passed, and she didn't get adopted. The little dog was adopted before her, even though he yapped so loudly it made my brain hurt. For some reason, people seemed put off by her.

And then I found out why.

Andi was usually the one to supervise the pet visits. When a family came over to adopt, she'd take the pet into our adoption room and let them all hang out, to see if they were a good fit. But one day Andi called in sick, and I had to supervise a visit between a family and Lucy.

I was feeling pretty good about it. It was a family of three: a mom, a dad, and a boy. The mother—who seemed to wear the pants in the family—was immediately attracted to Lucy. "Wow, what a beautiful dog," she said, looking into the cage. "And so calm, too. So quiet."

So I took Lucy out of her crate and led her to the adoption room, where the Robinsons were waiting. Then I took a seat in the corner and let the family interact with her.

That was when I finally realized why no one would adopt her.

She didn't *act* the way you'd expect a dog to. She didn't approach the family or lick their hands or wag her tail. She didn't cower away from them in fear, either. She simply walked into the corner of the room, sat down, and stared at them. With those cold blue eyes.

An awkward silence filled the room. Finally, the boy got up and cautiously approached the dog. He asked if he could pet her, and I nodded.

He pat her on the head a few times. At first, she ignored him. Then she slowly turned to look at him.

They stared at each other for a few seconds. Then the boy backed away.

They made a few other attempts to connect with Lucy. There were toys in the adoption rooms, and the mother squeezed a squeaky toy, trying to get her interested. No reaction. The boy grabbed a knotted rope for tug-of-war and held it in front of her, trying to get her to play. She didn't—she just stared at him.

The family left empty handed.

I led Lucy back to her room of isolation. And now, I noticed something I hadn't before. As I passed by our other animals on display, they reacted to her.

The mice scurried towards the opposite end of the cage, squeaking loudly.

The birds squawked and fluttered to different perches.

Even the fish seemed agitated, swimming back and forth in their tanks.

I led Lucy back to her crate. As I closed the door and secured the lock, she stared up at me with those ice-blue eyes. I felt a chill run down my spine.

Over the next few days, I tried to play with Lucy. Maybe she was just having trouble adjusting to the new environment.

I took her into the adoption room myself. I squeezed the squeaky toy. I shook the tug-of-war toy. I brought out some treats. But she just sat there, still as a statue, watching my every move with those bright blue eyes.

I took her for a walk on Tuesday afternoon, just in

the parking lot and on the sidewalk next to the road. She seemed completely disinterested in her surroundings. She didn't bark at the squirrel we passed. She didn't sniff the ground or pull at her leash. She just slowly walked by my side.

It was... unnerving. I felt like I was walking a robot. Or a human wearing a dog suit. It certainly didn't feel like I was walking a dog.

And when we passed another dog on the sidewalk, it had the same reaction to her as the other dogs at the store. It backed away from her, snarling, baring its teeth. Lucy didn't growl or bark back—she just stared at it.

She did react to one thing, though. About a half mile from the pet store, there's a small cemetery. As soon as we got close, Lucy began digging her paws into the cement. I gently tugged on her leash. "Come on, Lucy. Just a little further."

She didn't budge.

A chill went down my spine. Could she see something, sense something, that I couldn't? "Okay, okay," I told her. "We'll go back to the store."

As if she understood my words, she turned around and started heading back to the store.

I know my experience with dogs is limited. I haven't had a dog of my own in years. But I've never seen a dog act like her before. And I couldn't shake the feeling that there was something wrong with her.

Something terribly wrong.

When Andi got back to work, I asked her about Lucy. "Where did we get her, again?"

"She came from Brightview Rescue, I think. Why?"

"Doesn't she... freak you out a little bit?"

Andi laughed. "No?"

"She doesn't act normal. She just sits there and stares at everything."

"Dogs have different personalities," she said. "Some are loud, some are quiet. Some are friendly, some are shy. She's just one of the shier ones. But don't worry—she'll find the perfect family in no time."

I frowned. Andi was probably right—she had a lot more experience with dogs than I did. My family had a collie mix when I was a kid, but that was it. Andi had two dogs of her own at home, in addition to growing up around them. She also worked at the pet store a lot longer than I had.

I decided to call Brightview Rescue to find out more about Lucy. If I knew her family history, maybe I could understand why she was acting so strange. Maybe I'd even be able to help her. Who knows—maybe a subtle change to her environment, like moving her to a different room or giving her different toys, would make all the difference.

When I called, they transferred me to a guy named Michael. He'd apparently handled all of Lucy's stuff when she was there.

He told me a strange story.

First off, he couldn't give me her family history because he found her out in the woods. In the middle of nowhere.

Second, he described the exact same stuff we'd been dealing with. All the other dogs at the shelter barked and growled at her. A lot of people were interested in adopting her because she looked so unique, but they quickly lost interest when all she did was stare at them.

"I even had one guy ask me if she was a robot," he said, with a laugh. "Like, he actually thought we were trying to pass off some AI-robot dog as the real thing."

"And you don't know *anything* about where she came from?" I asked again.

Then he told me something that chilled me to the core.

When Michael first found her, he'd assumed she was a runaway. Even though she was a mile out into the woods, and didn't have a collar, she looked well cared for. She wasn't thin or dehydrated or anything. So he'd spent that first week combing the internet, and local bulletin boards, for a missing dog that looked like Lucy.

He found one.

He immediately called them up, telling them he'd found their dog. But they told him that couldn't be possible. Because their dog had already been found. Two weeks ago.

"This dog looked *exactly* like Lucy," Michael told me. "The photo could've easily been a photo of her.

Such a coincidence. I mean, she's a very unusual looking dog. To have two dogs that look like that, in the same town..." He went on and on about it for a while, and I had to agree with him. It was a very strange coincidence.

For a long time after I hung up the phone, I just stared at the wall. The more I learned about Lucy, the more uneasy I got. And I couldn't help but think, *there's something terribly wrong with this dog.*

That night, I found myself all alone in the store after closing time.

Andi and I had an agreement. She dealt with the reptiles, and I cleaned the grooming station after close. I've been afraid of snakes since I was a kid, so I was all too happy to sweep up dog hair for an hour if it meant I didn't have to deal with those things.

I headed towards the grooming station at the back of the store. Humming, I began to sweep up the mounds of dog and cat hair that had accumulated throughout the day.

I was almost done when I heard it.

Barking. Wild, frantic barking echoing through the pet store.

The hairs on my neck stood on end. I stood up and whipped around, scanning the store. From my vantage point, though, I couldn't see much.

Did someone break in?

That was the only possible explanation. But I'd

definitely locked the door after Andi left, and the alarm didn't go off.

I grabbed the only thing near me that could possibly be used as a weapon—a pair of sharp scissors—and headed down the aisle. The barking grew louder, more frantic, ringing in my ears. And that wasn't the only sound. From the aisle next to me, I heard the other animals: birds frantically screeching. Snakes hissing. Mice scampering wildly through their cages.

I took a deep breath, readying myself behind a display of cat food, and then turned the corner.

Nothing.

The front door was closed. The windows weren't broken. I let out the breath I'd been holding. There was no way anyone could be inside the store right now. We were located in a strip mall, so the only possible entry points were the front door, which I'd just checked, and the back door—which was near the grooming station.

I didn't know why the dogs were barking—but I was safe. I tucked the scissors into my pocket and turned around to finish cleaning.

That's when I saw it.

The door to Lucy's room was open.

Did she escape? I walked towards the door, my heart pounding in my chest. That's all I needed. For Lucy to pee in the middle of the store, or break open some dog food, or do something else that required another hour of cleanup.

But when I poked my head into the room, I

gasped.

The entire left wall of Lucy's cage had been broken off. It lay on the ground, slightly dented. And Lucy was nowhere to be found.

"Oh, for Pete's sake," I grumbled. "Lucy? Lucy, where are you?"

The animals had grown quiet now. The store was silent—dead silent. A chill ran down my spine. I stood frozen, listening for the click of dog nails on tile. "Lucy! I have treats for you!" I grabbed the box of treats off the shelf and shook it. "Here, girl!"

Nothing.

What kind of dog doesn't come for treats? All the other dogs would come running at the ol' treat shake.

I started to search the store, starting with the small pet aisle. I passed the snakes first, which were coiled up at the back of their cages. Forked tongues flicked out as they watched me, a few of them hissing. I continued, past the birds who eyed me warily, past the mice who burrowed deep in the pine shavings. It almost seemed like they were trying to hide.

"Lucy!" I called.

And then I froze.

There was a shadow in front of me. Stretching out further than my own. The hairs on the back of my neck stood on end. I felt the air shift behind me. Something was standing behind me—something *big*—and it wasn't Lucy.

"Wh-what do you want?" I asked, my voice shaking.

I wanted to turn around. But I didn't. What if they

were armed? The shadow was too blurry to make out well—but they were clearly someone much taller than me. I didn't stand a chance.

My hand slowly went into my pocket, feeling for my wallet. And my phone. I held both up, behind me. "Here. Take them. Please, don't hurt me." I had no idea how he got in. Maybe he picked the lock. But hopefully he would just take my stuff and go.

But he didn't take them.

Instead, I felt something wet against my hand. A *tongue.*

I yelped and jumped back. But it was just Lucy, standing there. Trying to pry the box of treats from my hand. I wheeled around—but the store was empty. No one was there. I looked down at the floor. The shadow was gone.

There was no way he could've disappeared that fast. Especially without making any sound. Hands shaking, I fed Lucy some of the treats. Then I led her back to her crate, jerry-rigged it with zipties, and closed the door.

I did a final loop around the store, but no one was there. Nothing was taken. Everything was as it should be. So I locked up and went home.

―――――――――

But when I got to the store the next morning, it was trashed.

Bags of food were torn open, spilling out onto the floor. Toys were ripped off their racks. Even the animals seemed on edge—the store was filled with squawks and squeaks and barks.

We thought there had been a break-in. Until we found Lucy at the back of the store, just chilling out. When I checked her room, I found the crate totally destroyed. The zipties held, but the opposite side had been busted open.

I stared at the mess of dented metal. It was hard to believe an 80-pound dog had done so much damage. It was also hard to believe that a dog had turned the doorknob and opened the door.

Our manager closed the store for the day. It took us nearly five hours to clean everything up. The damage was unbelievable. An empty fish tank had been shattered, scattering shards of glass all over the floor. More than ten bags of food had been ripped open. Even one of the lighting fixtures was smashed.

After cleaning, I decided to watch the security footage. Because I refused to believe that Lucy could do *all* of this damage.

We only have one security camera. It's right at the entrance to the store. You can only see the edge of one aisle, and a few of the fish tanks. So I knew I wasn't going to get full footage of Lucy destroying the store or anything.

I queued up the footage and hit PLAY.

Around 1:15 AM, Lucy escaped. I heard the door bang open from somewhere offscreen. Then I heard rustling sounds, and a loud *thump*. The one aisle in view of the camera shook—as if a huge weight had rammed into it.

I leaned into the screen, heart pounding. Our aisles are bolted into the floor—there's no way a dog could shake the aisle like that. It would probably take a two-hundred pound man, at the very least, ramming his entire body weight into the thing.

I watched as the aisle shook again. I heard a ripping sound, as bags of food were being torn open off-screen.

Then I saw a shadow.

An enormous shadow, stretching across the floor. Just like I'd seen last night. Bigger than Lucy. Bigger than *me*.

The aisle shook again. I swallowed.

And then the shadow got bigger.

They were coming closer to the camera. I held my breath, watching the edge of the screen, my heart pounding in my chest.

And then I saw it. Just for a split-second, I saw it.

A long, twisted, sinewy leg. Enormous, elongated claws. Gray skin—not fur.

And then it was gone.

I rewound the footage several times. But it was there. Something that didn't look like a dog's paw, or a human hand, or like anything I'd ever seen before.

But it was the exact same gray color as Lucy's fur.

———

I showed the footage to Andi and my manager. But they both had reasonably boring explanations. Andi thought someone *had* broken in, somehow, and was wearing a Halloween costume for kicks. It was getting to that time of year. My manager explained that the wide-angle lens stretched out everything near the edges of the screen, so it was Lucy's paw, just distorted by the camera.

Their theories made more sense than mine, I guess. I'm not even sure what my theory was. But there were too many strange things adding up about Lucy.

The next day, we re-opened for business. I went in to check on her and make sure the new cage was still holding up. We'd have to move her to another shelter soon. The room needed to be opened up for cat adoptions, and the other dogs didn't tolerate her, so we didn't really have an option.

I was relieved. I didn't want to deal with her anymore. All I could think of when I looked at her was that horrible gray claw, reaching out from the aisle. And I hated the way she sat still like that, just *staring* at me.

When I looked into those blue eyes... it felt like I was making eye contact with something far more intelligent than a dog.

"You're going to be out of here soon," I told her, patting the top of the cage. "You won't have to be here much longer. That's a good thing, right?"

She tilted her head, slowly, as if she understood me.

"And you'll get adopted by a nice family, and you'll get a whole big house to run around in. It'll be really good. I promise."

I tapped the cage again, then left the room. She watched me intently until I closed the door.

That night, it was just Andi and me closing up the store again. Her handling the snakes, me cleaning up the grooming station. She insisted on staying with me until I was ready to go, in case "the kid in the Halloween costume came back."

I just wanted this whole thing to be over. I wanted Lucy gone.

Five minutes before we officially closed, I heard the bells jingle at the front of the store.

Andi and I exchanged a look. Then I walked towards the front of the store. "We're closing in five minutes," I called out as I approached. The last thing I needed was some guy who'd spend a half hour choosing dog treats.

I rounded the corner, and there he was. He was tall—about six-foot-two—and very skinny, with curly blond hair. He looked like he was a few years older than me. He glanced at me, then past me, further into the store.

I immediately didn't like him. Something about him, about the way he was glancing around, made me uneasy. I swallowed, thinking about last night. "Can I help you?" I asked, in my most confident voice.

He paused. The silence stretched out for several seconds—then he finally spoke. "I'm looking for dog food."

"What type of dog food? We have canned, dry..."

"Anything's good," he replied.

That struck me as odd. Usually people know

exactly what they want for their dogs: brand, flavor, size. If this guy was good with any dog food, why didn't he just go to the Wess Market across the street? No need to come to the pet store. Especially because our stuff is usually marked up a bit.

I walked down the aisle, leading him to the section of dog food. "Here you go. Lots of choices."

He barely looked at them. Just grabbed one off the shelf and headed towards the cash register. *What a weird guy,* I thought. I headed towards the register—

Grrrrr.

A growl broke the silence. I whipped around—and realized it wasn't coming from the dog adoption room, but the Lucy's room.

In the weeks she'd been here, I'd *never* heard her growl.

I turned back towards the man. He was staring at Lucy's door—but as soon as he saw me looking, his eyes snapped back to me. "Can you hurry it up?" he asked, irritated. I grabbed the bag of food, scanned it, and slid it back across the counter.

But when I looked up, I was face-to-face with a gun.

"Open the register. Empty everything into the bag," he muttered.

My hands began to shake. I opened the register and grabbed the cash. There wasn't much, but I put it dutifully into the bag. My eyes never left the gun, pointed straight at my head. In my peripheral vision, I looked for Andi. But she must've still been in the back. I couldn't see her anywhere.

My fingers slipped over the money, my heart pounding in my chest, staring down the barrel of the gun.

And then I heard it.

Clang.

A loud, metallic sound. Coming from Lucy's room. The man's eyes flicked over to the door. "Is someone back there?"

I shook my head.

"If you're playing some kind of game with me—"

Bang.

The door flew open. I whipped around.

All the blood drained out of my face.

An enormous shape came into view. Gray, sickly skin. Long, thin legs—dozens of them—ending in huge claws. Its head was wolf-like, but when it opened its mouth, its rows and rows of razor-sharp teeth looked more like a shark's. And its eyes... there were several of them, slitted and inky black.

And they all focused on the man with the gun.

He turned white as a sheet. Then he turned around and ran out of the store, as fast as his legs could take him.

I backed away from the counter. The *thing* towered above me, its head brushing the ceiling. Its dozens of legs moved in synchrony like a spider crawling across the floor, heading towards its prey. I could hear Andi screaming now, somewhere behind me, but I couldn't turn away from the creature.

This is it. This is how I die.

I closed my eyes.

And then I felt a tongue licking my hand.

My eyes shot open and—there was Lucy. Dog Lucy. Standing in front of me, licking my hand.

I wheeled around. Andi was frantically calling the police, freaking out, crying. I was numb. My legs were weak.

"Lucy?" I whispered.

She just stared back at me with those bright blue eyes.

Andi and I told our manager about Lucy. She didn't believe us. Neither did the police. They did catch the guy who attempted the robbery, though, and he confessed to everything.

I cleaned out Lucy's room the next day. We needed the room for the cats. Besides, she couldn't stay here. She would continue to wreck the store and scare the other animals and do who knows what else.

So I adopted her.

Lucy and I have had a great time so far. She's been enjoying long walks, hanging around my apartment, and eating dinner scraps. I'm even trying to teach her how to play fetch. No luck yet. But we'll see.

I think, eventually, she will return to the woods. It is her home, after all. But for now... she's content sitting on the sofa with me, watching TV, and getting head pats.

And I don't mind the extra security. If anyone tries to break in, they'll get the scare of their lives.

DISTURBING YOUTUBE AD

After work, I do the exact same thing every day. I crack open a cold can of Diet Dr. Pepper, put my feet up, and watch an hour or two of funny videos on YouTube. I always plan to do something productive—cook a healthy dinner, go for a run, make progress on my paintings—but I never do. I'm always too exhausted from work to do anything else.

I don't think humans were built to work 8 hours a day. Sitting in the same room, at the same desk, in front of the same computer. I think we're just forced to accept this as the norm because greedy CEOs have *made* it the norm. But, I digress...

All you need to know is that tonight was no different than any other night. I popped the can open. Put my feet up. Opened my laptop.

Clicked on a funny YouTube video about the ridiculousness of *Twilight*.

But then I froze.

I'd expected an ad to pop up. Instead, there was a message over where the video should play—bold white letters over black.

> YOUR VIDEO WILL START SHORTLY!
> WOULD YOU LIKE TO VIEW A 15 SECOND AD,
> OR REMOVE 15 SECONDS FROM YOUR LIFE?

I squinted at the screen. *What?* I'd never seen anything like this. I looked down at where the progress bar would be, thinking it was actually an ad itself. But there wasn't any bar, and there wasn't a "Skip" button, either.

What is this?

After staring at it for a minute, I decided it must be some new thing YouTube was rolling out. Like when, instead of an ad, they show you some sort of poll. *Is this ad relevant to you? Have you ever bought anything from these companies? Help our sponsor by answering the following question...*

My mouse hovered over the two buttons. *15-SECOND AD. REMOVE 15 SECONDS OF LIFE.*

Out of curiosity, I clicked the latter.

The video started playing. Immediately—no ad. *Well, that's cool.* When the video was over, I popped some leftovers in the microwave, and started another video. Again, instead of an ad, I got the same prompt.

> YOUR VIDEO WILL START SHORTLY!
> WOULD YOU LIKE TO VIEW A 30 SECOND AD,
> OR REMOVE 30 SECONDS FROM YOUR LIFE?

I let out a little laugh and clicked on *REMOVE 30 SECONDS OF LIFE.*

The video started to play.

But only a few seconds into the video, I heard the microwave beep.

Already?

I put it on for one minute.

There's no way it's already done...

Confused, I paused the video and walked into the kitchen. The microwave had stopped its cycle. I pulled out the food out—and it was warm.

But it was only in there for like, ten seconds.

A sense of unease settled in my stomach. I picked up my bowl of mushy chicken alfredo and walked back to the computer. Then I clicked on another video.

YOUR VIDEO WILL START SHORTLY!

WOULD YOU LIKE TO VIEW A 30 SECOND AD, OR REMOVE 30 SECONDS FROM YOUR LIFE?

My cursor hovered over the REMOVE button.

But something stopped me. Something felt... off. *The food... it was almost like...* I shook my head. There was no way.

It was almost like I skipped ahead in time.

"That's impossible," I muttered to myself. But then I had an idea. I pulled out my phone, put it on the counter, and pulled up the stopwatch.

I hit the stopwatch—

Then I immediately clicked *REMOVE 30 SECONDS OF LIFE*.

The video started immediately.

But when I looked down at the stopwatch, my heart dropped.

It read *32 seconds*.

Nonono. There was no *way* thirty seconds had gone by. I *just* clicked the button, a few seconds ago.

What the fuck?!

My heart pounded in my ears. I glanced around the room. Then I tried it again. My finger shook as I lowered it onto the phone screen.

Tap. Click.

The stopwatch read *32 seconds.*

But it didn't feel like 30 seconds. It felt like two seconds. Anxiety slipped into me like lead, weighing me down. My legs felt weak.

I picked up the phone and texted my friend Chris.

Can you come over? Or can I come over to your place? I need to talk to someone.

I waited for a few minutes. He didn't reply.

It was late. Almost 10. I set the phone down and stared at the paused video, my heart pounding.

And then I had another idea.

I set my phone down on a shelf across from me. Propped it up against some books. Pressed the RECORD button. Then I walked back over to my desk, sat down, and clicked on another YouTube video.

YOUR VIDEO WILL START SHORTLY!

WOULD YOU LIKE TO VIEW A 60 SECOND AD,

OR REMOVE 60 SECONDS FROM YOUR LIFE?

60 seconds now?! I sucked in a deep breath. Glanced up at the phone, the black eye of the camera looking down at me.

My cursor hovered over the 'REMOVE' button.

I clicked.

The video immediately began to play.

I got up and walked over to the phone. Picked it up and stopped the recording.

The length of the video was 1 minute, 17 seconds.

What. The. Fuck.

I went over to the sink and splashed water on my face. Checked the clock a few times, pinched myself, to make sure I wasn't dreaming. Then I picked my phone back up.

The recording was still there.

All one minute, seventeen seconds of it.

This is so fucking weird.

I sat back down. Then I opened the video and, with a deep breath, pressed PLAY.

I watched myself walk over to the seat in front of the computer. Then I sat down. I held my breath as my fingers went to the touchpad, clicking the REMOVE button.

Click.

Video-me stared at the computer screen. With incredible intensity—like I was watching the most riveting thing I'd ever seen in my life. My mouth hung slightly open, and my normally fidgety hands were still on the desk. I was just *staring,* with everything in me.

At first, no audio came out of the computer's speakers. I was expecting a loud jingle for an insurance company, or a chirpy female voice telling me about laundry detergent, but it was just silence.

Until, ten seconds in, I heard a high-pitched whine.

It sounded like the noise old TVs make when you

leave them on. Or ringing in your ears. A mechanical tone so high-pitched it's almost out of the range of human hearing.

And when the tone sounded, video-me's hands flew to the keyboard.

And they began feverishly typing.

I stood there, frozen, watching the video. Watching my fingers race across the keyboard. My eyes staring at the screen with absolute concentration. My mouth still hanging open. I thought I could see a silvery strand of drool falling from my lips, onto the desk.

What the actual fuck?

I briefly glanced away from the phone, to my desk—and noticed a small puddle of liquid shining in the low light.

What was I typing?

Was the ad, or whatever YouTube was showing me… was it MAKING me do this?

Because I looked dazed. Hypnotized. Controlled.

As the video approached its end, I saw video-me snap out of it. I closed my mouth. My hands started to fidget. I got out of the seat and walked towards the phone on the shelf.

And that was it.

I stood there, frozen, the silence ringing in my ears. *This is crazy. Absolutely insane.* It was conspiracy-level stuff—YouTube is mind-controlling people through ads that erase time! Quick, block YouTube on every device that you own!

If I had been on anything—hell, if I'd even had a

glass of wine—I would've blamed it on that in an instant. But I was stone-cold sober.

I walked back over to the computer and put my hand on the screen, about to close it.

But then I paused.

I couldn't see the computer screen in the video—it was the wrong angle. But if I put the phone behind me, I could see what I was typing.

No. You're not doing that again, my inner voice instantly protested. *Close the laptop and get out of here.*

But I couldn't. Curiosity was tugging at me—I had to know what I was doing. I quickly propped the phone up behind me and sat back down at the computer.

I clicked on another video.

YOUR VIDEO WILL START SHORTLY!

WOULD YOU LIKE TO VIEW A 60 SECOND AD,

OR REMOVE 60 SECONDS FROM YOUR LIFE?

I took a deep, shuddering breath.

Then I clicked REMOVE.

The video instantly began to play. But I knew that was just from my point of view. I grabbed my phone from behind me and, sure enough—the recording time read 1 minute, 6 seconds.

I swallowed.

And then I hit PLAY.

What I saw was so ridiculous that I should've laughed. It should've been the funniest thing I saw all week. But instead I stared at the screen, my heart plummeting further and further.

Where the ad had been, there was instead a

textbox. In it, I was typing the same six words, over and over.

I WANT TO BUY SPARKLE DETERGENT.
I WANT TO BUY SPARKLE DETERGENT.
I WANT TO BUY SPARKLE...

I must've written it fifty times before the minute was up. Then the textbox disappeared, and the video started to play. I watched video-me get up, turn around, and turn off the recording.

I slammed the laptop shut and went straight to bed, my heart racing in my chest. When I couldn't sleep, pulled out my phone and began searching for this phenomenon. Typing keywords into Google like, *weird youtube ad, youtube remove 30 seconds from life,* etc.

Nothing came up.

But it doesn't end there.

Because I could've sworn it was around 2:30 AM when I started searching. And I could've sworn I spent no more than a half hour Googling.

But when I checked the time after closing out of all my tabs, it was nearly *four* AM.

I think I lost an entire hour.

And I have no way of finding out what happened —what I was typing, or watching, or being brainwashed to buy—in that hour.

THE HEADLESS JOGGER

I don't know what to do. This is going to sound completely, batshit insane. But I have to tell someone.

About a week ago, I saw a jogger on my way home from work. We live in a small town with a lot of sidewalks, so it's pretty common to see joggers or people walking their dogs after dark. Sometimes they'll get creative with the lights—I've seen dog leashes strung with LEDs, people wearing headlamps. This is especially common now, in winter, when the sun sets before 5 pm.

So, I thought nothing of it. A pinprick of light, bobbing up and down the sidewalk, about thirty yards ahead of me. Just another jogger.

But then I got closer. And I realized the way the light was bobbing was… strange. I couldn't really put my finger on why it was strange; it just was. Something in my brain clicked—*it doesn't look like it should.*

And then, as I passed him, my entire body froze.

He had no head.

I know. I couldn't be sure; I only saw him for a second. As soon as my brain registered it, he'd already passed. I glanced at the rearview mirror and saw the bobbing light receding, but it was too dark to see whether he had a head or not.

As I drove home, I struggled to find a reasonable explanation for what I'd seen. Maybe he'd been wearing a balaclava—it was pretty cold out. That would render his face nearly invisible in the darkness. *Wouldn't I still see his eyes, though? Or, something?* Or could he have been wearing some sort of costume, some sort of mask? But why? It wasn't anywhere near Halloween.

Well, whatever it was—there was no way he was actually headless.

It's easy to see things. Not hallucinations, but little glitches in your brain, misinterpreting reality. Like when a bit of hair falls in front of your eyes, and you think it's a shadow person for a second. Or when you see a misshapen tree stump by the road, and think it's a deer. I remember the time I convinced myself Santa was real, even though I was too old to believe, because I'd seen a shadow in the neighbor's front yard on Christmas Eve. When it was probably just a bush, or a deer, or even a piece of my hair in my peripheral vision.

By the time I was at the front door, I'd completely convinced myself that it wasn't a headless jogger.

"I scared myself so bad tonight," I told my husband over dinner. "On the way home, I saw this jogger, and I thought—I thought he didn't have a head."

My husband laughed. "The Headless Horseman trying to lose a little weight, huh?"

I chuckled.

"Maybe you'll see him at Dawn Yoga next. Doing a downward-facing dog." He took a bite of garlic bread. "Or, hey, movie idea. *The Headless Horseman* for 2024. Ichabod Crane goes on TikTok and finds a headless fitness guru. They could call it... *The Headless Influencer.*"

"Oh my gosh," I laughed, rolling my eyes.

But that was before things got worse.

On Tuesday night, I took our dog out for a walk after work. And about halfway down the street, I saw it: a light, in the distance, bobbing up and down. I crossed to the other side of the street, to get out of his way.

Something felt wrong about it, though. That same sense of wrong I couldn't place when I saw the light on the headless jogger. But I continued down the street as he grew closer.

And that's when Sadie started to growl.

She stared at the light. Ears pinned back, teeth bared, growling. My stomach dropped. "It's okay, girl," I said, but the pit in my stomach grew.

I tried to walk forward, but Sadie wouldn't budge. So I stood there, phone in hand, pressed against the curb as the light got closer. And closer, and closer...

Until he came into view.

The jogger's pale arms swung with each step. His

feet hit the pavement with a rhythmic *thump, thump, thump*. The light shone from something strapped to his wrist, erratically bouncing off the asphalt.

Thump, thump, thump. Closer.

I held my breath, staring at the spot above his shoulders. Fifteen feet away, now... ten...

No.

He had no head.

It was obvious this time. Absolutely clear. There was nothing above his shoulders but thin air. Yet his body was still pumping away, his feet pounding the asphalt. I stared at him, petrified with fear, not even understanding what I was seeing. Sadie let out a snarl.

Then he passed me.

And I saw something else.

The muscles in his exposed shoulder. In the short, smooth stump of his neck. They *moved*. As if...

He was turning to look at me.

I yanked on Sadie's leash, and this time she had no problem running. We sprinted back to the house, both of us panting, terrified. As soon as I got inside I locked every lock we had, even the deadbolt we rarely used.

"Steven!" I screamed.

I told him what happened, tripping over my own words, blabbering, barely coherent. Not knowing what else to do, he called the police. They came over and searched the neighborhood; but they didn't find any headless jogger.

Of course they didn't.

The three of us packed up and went to my sister's for the night, just an hour away. I couldn't sleep at home. *It was on our street.* Maybe it even followed me home, knew where we lived. I knew that sounded crazy. But I had seen it, and I would swear on my own life that there was a headless man running around out there.

As I stared at the ceiling, trying to fall asleep, a childhood memory popped in my head. A lesser known Dr. Seuss story that I had loved as a kid. *What was I scared of?,* it was called. A pair of "pale green pants, with nobody inside them" follows and torments the main character. It has a happy ending, of course, but the biting unease of seeing something that's so empty, that doesn't have a head or any place to put intelligence or a brain or a soul—yet is moving, acting like something sentient—stuck with me.

It felt oddly similar to the feeling I had now, dialed up to 100.

We spent two nights at my sister's place, but after that, we had to get home. The extra commute time was wearing on both of us, and my sister's one-year-old was waking us up at night. So we headed back home, and I tried to pretend like I'd never seen the headless jogger. Maybe that was the last time I'd ever see him.

It wasn't.

Because at 3 AM that night, I woke with a start. And when I rolled over, I saw a light twinkling in through the blinds.

What the hell...

Without thinking, I pulled up the blinds.
No.
My blood ran cold. I stood there, frozen, my feet stuck to the floor. I couldn't move. Couldn't think.

I was face-to-face—or rather face-to-nothing—with the headless jogger.

It was just *standing there,* six feet outside my window. Still as a statue.

The blinds clattered shut. When I finally had the courage to peer through them, it was gone.

I'm terrified. I don't know what this thing wants, or what it wants to do to me. I don't even know how it's *thinking.* How it's moving. I went to the police again, but no one will believe me. My husband is suggesting a vacation, just the two of us. He thinks I'm going crazy.

I'm not.

So, please—if you ever see a jogger at night, and you think for a second they don't have a head—

Don't brush it off as a brain glitch.

Run the other way, and don't look back.

I HACKED A RING CAMERA

It was just supposed to be a stupid prank.

You know how some people can hack into Ring cameras? My friend Johnny is a computer whiz, and he thought it would be the funniest shit to scare someone senseless by spying on them and talking out of the microphone.

In retrospect, it was a terrible idea. Even at the time, it felt sort of gross. But we're 15 years old. Besides, Eddie was on board, and I didn't want to be the party-pooper telling them we should like, *not break the law and spy on people*. That would be totally lame. Right?

It took about an hour for Johnny to hack into the camera. The account was registered to a guy who lived over a thousand miles away, in Texas. The three of us huddled around the computer as the live feed loaded.

"What if it's like, people having sex?"

"Score!"

"Dude, no one would set up the camera in their *bedroom.*"

"Who said they'd be in the bedroom?!"

We were cut off by the video feed filling the screen.

For ten whole minutes, it was just an empty kitchen. Completely boring. It looked like a rich kitchen though, with all that stuff you see in Home Depot, that my mom would drool over every time we went.

We waited. Eddie opened a bag of chips and started eating. "Sssshhh, they'll hear you!" Johnny hissed.

A few more minutes went by. Finally, a shadow appeared on the wall. Then a woman walked into view.

Much to our disappointment, she wasn't hot. She was older, about sixty or so, with blonde hair cut into a severe bob. Looked rich from her clothing and stuff. She was looking back into the hallway, talking to someone off-screen.

"What's she saying?" Eddie whispered.

"Sssssshh!"

We listened, and finally, I could make out a few snippets of her words.

"leave it here tonight..."

"deal with it tomorrow..."

"in the freezer..."

Johnny leaned towards the computer, a wicked

grin on his face. He opened his mouth to yell something into the microphone—

But at that moment, someone else came on screen.

It was a man. But he didn't look like he was her husband—he looked like he was half her age, and a foot taller, than her. A buff guy. The type of guy you wouldn't want to meet in a dark alley late at night.

His pale blue eyes swept across the kitchen. Then he stepped in front of the fridge. "The freezer?" he asked, his low voice clearly audible.

She nodded.

He opened the left side of the fridge, presumably the freezer, and began pulling everything out of it. Not just the food, but the shelving and the drawers. Like my mom does when she's doing a deep clean.

Finally, he stood up, brushed off his pants, and walked back out of the kitchen.

When he came back... he was dragging something behind him.

I stared at the screen, my heart pounding. A large, long object in a black trashbag slid over the kitchen floor behind him. He stopped in front of the fridge for a moment—then he crouched down. With a grunt, he lifted the *thing* upright and began trying to shove it into the freezer.

Johnny, Eddie, and I looked at each other, our mouths hanging open. I knew we were all thinking the same thing.

Is that a body?

The man gave the thing another good shove—but

instead of fitting into the freezer, it fell back out towards him. He dodged, and it fell on the ground with a sickening *thwack*.

But in the fall, the trash bag shifted.

And poking out of the bag was a bloody, pale hand.

Johnny, Eddie, and I screamed. But as soon as the sound left my lips, I remembered—

The microphone is on.

Their heads snapped towards us. A pause.

"Was that coming from the camera?" she muttered to the man.

"Someone... someone might've hacked your camera. It happens," he replied. He sounded fearful.

But the woman didn't show an ounce of fear. She ran to the camera, her entire face filling the screen, jowls jiggling, wrinkled lips pressed together. Her hard, dark eyes stared into the camera—even though she couldn't see us.

And then she spoke.

"If you tell a soul about what you saw, I'll rip your fucking heads off."

Then she picked up the camera. The feed filled with blurry, twisted shapes as it was tilted around—and then everything went black.

I stared at Johnny and Eddie, shaking. By the time I looked back at the computer, we'd been logged out of the account.

———————

It's been three months since that happened. I eventually did tell the police—well, my parents did—but I don't remember the name on the account. And Johnny hasn't been able to log back in. Apparently, he got their info from a data breach at another company, and now that they've changed their password, he doesn't have a chance. He did pass along the email that was linked to the account, though.

So far, we've heard nothing from the police—or the woman. But I'm terrified. Because just a few days ago, my parents decided to get a Ring camera for our front door.

And when I got back from school yesterday—

I could've *sworn* I heard something come through the microphone, for just a second.

GARDEN HOSE

My hose grows longer every day. And no, that's not a euphemism. I'm literally talking about my garden hose, the one I ordered from Amazon, attached to the spigot by our deck.

At first, I didn't really notice it. Like a frog in slowly boiling water, the changes were so incremental, I didn't realize what was happening. A few weeks after buying the hose, it was a little easier to reach the kale patch at the far end of our garden. A few weeks after that, I could do it without pulling the hose taut.

I think the first time I really noticed it was about two weeks ago. I realized that, while watering the kale, the hose wasn't even in a straight line. It was all twisted and looped around the garden.

What?

"Did you put in a new hose or something?" I asked my wife, even though I knew the chances of her doing so were approximately zero.

"No. Why?"

I shook my head. "It just seems different... nevermind."

I grabbed a tape measure and walked back outside. I knew I'd bought a 25-foot hose. I stretched the hose out in a near-perfect line, then kneeled in the damp grass, starting to measure it.

"What are you *doing?*"

I glanced back to see Sara standing behind me.

"I'm, uh, measuring the hose."

"Why?"

"Thinking about putting in another raised bed over there," I said, pointing past the kale.

"*Another* one?"

"Maybe."

She lingered for a moment, sighed, and walked back inside. As soon as she was out of sight, I went back to measuring.

I couldn't believe it.

The hose measured 32 feet, 4 inches.

No. Maybe the manufacturer measured wrong. Maybe I got a defective one.

But I couldn't deny it. I *knew* it seemed to be growing longer and longer. Every day, I could reach a little bit further into the backyard.

I stepped back and took a photo of it. That night, I didn't roll it up—I left it stretched out in a line, with the terminus a few feet past the edge of the garden bed. The next morning, I took another picture, and compared them.

My blood ran cold.

The end of the hose was about six inches past where it was in the first photo.

It's growing.

No. That sounded crazy. A garden hose—*growing?* I ran back in and grabbed the tape measure. Got on my hands and knees, measured.

32 feet, 9 inches.

"Sara," I told my wife, finally. "You're going to think I'm crazy, but... I think our hose is... *growing.*"

"Huh?"

"Look. See?" I flipped through the two photos on my phone, showing her the difference. "The hose is longer in that one. I measured it, too. Five inches."

She gave me a *look*. Like I was acting totally insane.

I tried to tell her a few more times, but she didn't believe me. A few days passed, and I started to panic. At the beginning, the hose seemed to only be growing by the inch; just a little easier to reach the kale patch every day. Now it was growing by the foot. For Pete's sake, it nearly reached the woods now.

I brought Sara out and forced her to measure the hose. She was annoyed, but I didn't care. "If you do this, and you still don't believe me, I won't bring it up anymore."

"Okay. Thirty-seven feet... three inches?"

"Write it down."

"What?"

"Or email it to yourself, or something. Don't forget that number."

She gave me another *look*, but wrote down the

number on the fridge whiteboard. The next morning, I made her come out with me, and measure it again.

Her eyes went wide as she read off the number.

"Thirty-nine feet... eight inches."

"See? I told you."

"But that's impossible. Maybe... maybe I measured wrong—"

"By more than two feet?"

She just shook her head.

We stared at each other for a moment, not sure what to say. Not willing to speak into words this ridiculous thing, that made no logical sense. "Let's... let's just get rid of it," she said, finally.

We walked over to the hose bib. I bent down to unscrew it. The plastic of the hose felt strangely... *warm...* in my hands. Even though this part of the house was in shadow most of the day.

I twisted once. Twice. Three times.

"It's stuck on," I said, my heart starting to pound.

Sara ran inside. She came out with her huge chef's knife. And without a word, my 5' 2" wife, who's never shown aggression towards anyone or anything, knelt down and began hacking away at it.

"Sara—"

"Got it," she said, handing me the end of the hose. "Now get rid of it."

"I guess... I'll just throw it out?"

"No. Garbage day isn't until Thursday. Put it in a dumpster, or drop it in the woods, or something."

Both of those things were semi-illegal, but Sara was right. We weren't going to have this hose in a garbage bag in our garage for a few days. I imagined it growing and growing, stretching the plastic of the bag... until it broke free, slithered up the stairs, and strangled us in our sleep...

"I'll dump it somewhere." I started for the driveway.

"John?"

I turned around.

Sara's hands were covered in blood.

"Did you cut yourself?!"

I dropped the hose and helped her inside. Put her hands under the faucet. The rust-colored water swirled down the drain.

But when the water had washed the blood away, there wasn't a cut. Her hands were perfectly fine. I walked back out to the driveway, picked up the hose, and started for the car.

That's when I noticed it.

The hose... was bleeding.

Well, not *really,* but there was some dark liquid at the cut end that was smearing off on my hands too. It was dark and reddish-brown—rust, not blood. Because that would be ridiculous, blood coming from a hose.

But when I brought the cut section up to my face, I saw something was wrong with it—*horribly* wrong. The plastic cross-section, which should have been green like the exterior of the hose, was instead... a deep reddish-brown, like the liquid. And it wasn't uniform—it was striated with pinkish streaks.

Almost like... meat?

No. That was ridiculous. Just some new plastic they're using. Lots of hoses use recycled plastic on the interior, and a new layer on the inner and outer layers to prevent chemical leaching. That's the recycled plastic. Of course it's a weird color, of course it isn't uniform. It's all melted and cobbled together.

I threw the hose into the trunk. Then I drove around, but it looked like all the dumpsters at various shopping centers were either locked or cordoned off with chainlink fence. So I drove to a nearby park, walked a quarter mile into the woods, and dumped it off there.

Which was littering, but at that point, I didn't care.

I thought that was the end of our troubles. That we'd never see the hose again, and everything would go back to normal. I even thought it was more likely that we'd find ourselves in the plot of some B-rate horror movie, the hose slithering out of the woods like a snake, intent on strangling us to death.

What actually happened was far worse.

Sara got the symptoms first. Intense stomach pain and chills. Then it was me, running a dangerously high fever. We rushed to the ER, and the doctor told us the horrible news—

"All the symptoms line up with intestinal parasites."

And I can't help but think about all the produce we ate from the garden.

Watered with that hose.

It was a crazy theory. A parasite couldn't be

absorbed by a plant and then show up again in the fruit, and eaten. But I can't stop picturing water flowing through that tube of what looked like *meat*.

Watering our food.

Suffusing into our bodies.

Contaminating us with something unknown.

THERE'S SOMETHING WRONG WITH THIS HOSPITAL

Tonight, I started working as an ER doctor for Elmdale Memorial Hospital. The night shift wasn't my first choice, but we needed the extra money. My wife is on bed rest with a high-risk pregnancy right now, carrying a little boy due in three weeks.

But now, I wish I'd never taken the job. Because there is something horribly wrong with the patients here.

On my first night of the job, it was storming. Rain pelted down on the windshield, blurring the view of the hospital in front of me. But I saw enough: it was a depressing, stark building of concrete and dark glass. Almost resembling a prison more than a hospital.

I parked and made my way towards the entrance. But as I approached the emergency room, I noticed something strange: one floor of the hospital was completely dark. I couldn't tell if it was the third or the fourth floor, from where I was standing.

Maybe the storm cut some of the power, I thought. *But why would it only be one floor?*

Well, whatever the cause, it wouldn't be my problem. I worked on the first floor. Still, it was an ominous sight: a row of windows, completely dark, while all the other windows glowed bright against the rain. A vein of lightning shot across the sky, followed by the low rumble of thunder.

I took a deep breath and stepped into the building.

From the moment I stepped in, though, something seemed... off. For one, the emergency room was completely empty. It was so quiet, you could hear a pin drop—I didn't hear any beeping machines, or conversations, or people walking around. It was only seven o'clock, so it wasn't the dead of night or anything like that.

I walked into the triage area. "Hello?" I called.

Dr. Harris had given me a quick tour of the hospital during the orientation process. There were five triage rooms, where patients were kept before being admitted or released. I turned around, listening for footsteps, voices, anything.

"Hello?" I called again.

The curtain covering the room next to me billowed outwards. Then a silhouette pressed into the fabric, the cloth stretching over an unseen face. I leapt back, my heart pounding—but then the curtain was pushed aside and a nurse stepped out. "You must be Dr. Ramirez," she said, giving me a bright smile.

I nodded. "Where... is everybody?"

"Resting up for the night rush."

"The... night rush?"

"Nobody ever comes in now. Things get busy after midnight." She gave me another smile and then walked away.

What she said struck me as weird. We were in a small town, where most things closed at 9 or 10 PM. It wasn't like Elmdale Memorial Hospital was suddenly going to be flooded with drunk partygoers at 3 AM. I wanted to ask her more, but she was already halfway down the hallway.

I found the on-call room and decided to hang out there until I was needed. I stayed there, browsing on my phone, for about an hour before a different nurse came in and told me I was needed. It was an easy case: a man who'd accidentally cut himself while prepping dinner. I gave him a few stitches, and then it was back to twiddling my thumbs in the on-call room.

Around 10 o'clock, I took my dinner break. After eating my sad, lumpy sandwich, I decided to look for a vending machine. I'm a total sucker for junk food, despite what I tell my patients about eating healthy. I wandered away from triage and down the hallway, in search of an ice-cold coke and a pack of vinegar chips.

But, strangely, the hospital was even more empty over here.

The hallway was completely silent. Only my own footsteps echoed against the linoleum. There was a nurse's station ahead of me, but as I approached, I found it empty. All the computer screens were dark. And all the doors were closed in this wing of the hospital, with no light coming from underneath the doors.

Well. Nothing strange about that, really. Just meant the hospital wasn't filled to capacity. And that was a good thing, right?

I turned around, ready to give up on my quest for junk food.

And that's when I saw her.

A young woman was stumbling down the hallway. She was in bad shape. Her face was pale, white as a sheet. Her hair long hair was matted with sweat, sticking to her face, and she held both hands against her stomach. She let out a keening wail of pain.

"Do you need help?"

She didn't turn to look at me. "It hurts," she groaned finally, tears streaming down her face. "Hurts so much."

I grabbed her arm and turned her around, heading back towards the emergency room. *Where had she come from?* "Hey, we need some help!" I called out, but only my own voice echoed back.

How'd she get all the way back here? She wasn't wearing a hospital gown, or an ID bracelet. Which meant she hadn't even been seen yet. The emergency room entrance was impossible to miss—what back door had she taken to end up all the way out here?

But I didn't have much time to think. The woman's hand tore away from mine and she crumpled to the floor, wailing in pain, clutching her abdomen.

I sprang into action. After searching a few of the

empty rooms, I found an unused stretcher. I helped her onto it and then pushed her down the hallway as fast as I could.

In just a few minutes, we were back in the triage area. I got her settled into bed and then asked her as much as I could. Her name was Hayley Johnson, and she was 24. She told me she was in extreme abdominal pain: so much pain, it felt like someone was stabbing her in her right side, over and over. Two thoughts instantly occurred to me: appendicitis, or ectopic pregnancy.

I immediately gave the order for an ultrasound. Then I began sending the orders for surgery to the rest of the staff. As I was walking back to the room to check on her, though, someone called my name.

I turned around to see Dr. Harris running towards me. "Hey!" he shouted at me. "You're supposed to clear any surgical procedures with me first!"

"Sorry, I forgot." I started to turn away from him, thinking that was the end of our interaction.

"I'm canceling the surgery," he said behind me.

I turned around. "What?"

"You heard me. I'm canceling the surgery. I don't approve it."

I stared at him, my heart pounding. He was going to risk the life of that poor woman to prove some point? "You can't do that! She'll *die*! You'll—you'll be sued for malpractice!"

I was shouting, now. Some of the nurses turned to look in our direction. I swallowed, backing away slightly.

Dr. Harris leaned forward. He lowered his voice—and somehow his voice, his near-whisper, was more terrifying than if he started screaming at me. "You better not raise your voice to me *ever* again. She doesn't need surgery. She doesn't have appendicitis, or an ectopic pregnancy, or anything else. If you don't believe me, check the ultrasound."

Then he turned on his heel and hurried away.

The nurses quickly went back to their work, pretending they hadn't just been staring at us. I swallowed. I was *so* angry—but my anger had gotten me in trouble before. *Focus on Hayley,* I told myself. *She needs me right now.* I hurried back to her room.

The ultrasound tech was already in there. But when her eyes fell on me, she acted just as strangely as Dr. Harris. "You know, my time is valuable," she snapped. "You think you can just order people around to do whatever you want because you're a fancy hotshot *doctor,* but this isn't funny."

"What?"

"You know *exactly* what she is. We all do. You're just wasting my time." Huffing, she began wheeling the ultrasound cart out the door.

*What she **is**?* I thought. *Doesn't she mean... what she **has**?* "If you won't do the ultrasound, then I will," I said, grabbing the other end of the cart.

She shrugged and gave it to me, then left the room.

I'd only done a few ultrasounds before, back in medical school. After fiddling with the controls for a few minutes, I finally got it working. Hayley was only semi-conscious now, tossing and turning in the small hospital bed, groaning in pain.

I spread the gel on her abdomen and then lowered the probe. The ultrasound screen filled with white and black shapes, shifting and turning as I moved the probe across her belly. I continued searching, looking for the right spot, but I was rusty at this. I moved the probe further right—

And stopped dead.

In the middle of the screen was a pointed, white object. Glowing brightly against the grainy black-and-white shapes. *What... is that?*

I stared at it for a moment, scowling, the probe still on her belly. Then I sighed, pinching my nose, and glanced up.

My eyes caught on the window. On her reflection.

All the air sucked out of my lungs.

In the reflection... Hayley's clothes were soaked in blood. The hilt of knife stuck out of her stomach, glinting in the fluorescent light. Her eyes rolled up in her head, pure-white, from the pain. Her mouth gaped open in a never-ending scream.

And she was staring right at me.

I leapt out of the seat. The ultrasound probe clattered to the floor. My heart pounded in my chest and I backed away, the room spinning around me, wind rushing in my ears—

But then I realized Hayley looked exactly as she did before. Semi-conscious, groaning, laying in the hospital bed.

I need to get help.

I ran out of the room, calling for the nurses, the other doctors, anyone. But when I led them back into the room, rambling on like a crazy person... Hayley was gone.

No. She couldn't even walk. There's no way she could've gone anywhere.

Did Dr. Harris... take her somewhere?

"She was right there," I told them. "Did... did someone take her away?"

"What was her name?" one of the nurses asked.

"Hayley Johnson."

As soon as I said her name—the entire energy of the room changed. Like a wall had been put up between me and them. Like they knew something I didn't. One of the nurse's eyes got really wide, and then she hurried away. Dr. Stein shook her head, scoffing.

And then I was standing there, alone, in an empty hospital room.

For a few minutes, I didn't know what to do. But then I realized—if Hayley had been moved somewhere, it should be in the system. I ran over to the computer on the desk and typed in *Haley Johnson.*

I clicked on her record—and my blood turned to ice.

Hayley Johnson. Age 24. Admitted to the ER, after her boyfriend stabbed her with a hunting knife.

Four years ago.

No. That doesn't make any sense. It must be a different Hayley Johnson. It was a common name. Or maybe I'd gotten the patient's name wrong. Maybe *Hayley* was spelled different, like *Hailey* or *Hayleigh*. Maybe her last name was *Johns* or *Jones* or something else.

I tried typing different combinations of names into the system, but either no records came up, or they were a different age. I tried until my eyes ached and everything was blurry. I held my head in my hands. I was so tired.

I must've imagined what I'd seen in the window. What I'd seen on the ultrasound.

Or maybe I'm dreaming right now.

But then, as I stared blankly at the file, I noticed there was a little arrow in the bottom corner. When I clicked it, a second page came up. With just one sentence:

Transferred to floor 4.

It didn't say what date she was transferred. If it was four years ago, or now. But it was worth it to check. Maybe I could help her. I walked out of the room, my heart pounding, and went back down the hallway to the elevator. The doors whooshed open and I stepped inside. I pressed the button marked '4' and the elevator lurched underneath me.

1... 2... 3... 4.

Ding.

The doors began to open—and I realized something was horribly wrong.

The hospital wing in front of me was pitch black. The only light came from the elevator, spilling out into the darkness. "Hello?" I called out.

Only silence answered me.

This must've been the floor I'd seen from the

outside. The dark row of windows, without a single light. *The file must've been a mistake. This place looks abandoned. I'll try floor 3.* I pressed the button to close the elevator doors.

Nothing happened.

And then, with a sizzling *click*—the elevator light went out.

Every muscle in my body froze. It was absolutely pitch black—there was no light, from anywhere, not even from a glowing EXIT sign. There were no sounds, either. No ambient creaks or murmurs from the HVAC system. Just... nothing.

Hands trembling, I reached into my pocket and pulled out my phone. Using it as my light, I found the emergency button in the elevator and pressed it. Nothing happened. I took one step out of the elevator, lifting my phone up to illuminate my surroundings. My light didn't travel very far, but I could make out a long hallway, with doors on either side.

If this floor was like the others, the stairwell was on the opposite end of the hallway. I shuddered—but I didn't really have a choice. It was either wait here, for an undetermined amount of time, until someone came up to help. Or man up, walk down the hallway, and use the stairwell.

I started to walk.

I tried to think happy thoughts as I walked through the darkness, my flashlight bouncing up and down ahead of me. But the atmosphere was just too strange. Hospitals had emergency generators, because so many life-saving technologies depended on electricity. Why would they just leave the power off here? Maybe it was being renovated, or something—but when I looked around, I didn't see any evidence of that. No tarps or drills or cans of paint around.

In fact, this floor looked like it had been used recently. There was a stretcher parked outside room 12. A hospital gown was bunched up on the floor, stained with something dark. Even a tray of metal tools stood in the hallway, just out there in the open—with sharp, dangerous instruments like scalpels and forceps glinting in the light. It was like all the people working on this floor suddenly just... evaporated. Leaving everything behind.

As I continued through the darkness, however, I realized some of the doors ahead of me were open.

My blood turned to ice. I stopped in my tracks. *Just walk past them,* I told myself. And finally, after much convincing, I took a step.

The first door was only open a few inches. But there was light inside: flashing, bluish light, like there was a TV on. *I thought there wasn't any power up here,* I thought. As I passed it, I thought I heard the low murmur of canned laughter coming from its speakers.

Keep going.

The second door was on my left. It was pitch black, the inside an abyss of darkness. I swallowed, my throat dry. I approached it slowly; my legs felt like they were moving through molasses.

But as I approached, I heard something.

A soft moan of pain.

I should've just run the hell out of there. But a

little voice wormed its way into my head: *what if that's Hayley? What if she needs my help?*

I stopped outside the doorway and shined my light in.

The room was small. A cheap foldout table in one corner. An empty, filthy-looking bed in the middle. And a white curtain hanging from the ceiling, partitioning the room in two.

"Hello?" I called out.

The moan sounded again. From behind the curtain.

I took another step into the room, holding my phone up high. My legs shook underneath me. "Hayley?" I asked.

And then it happened.

The curtain rippled.

Something pointed, like a finger, slowly traced its way across the cloth. And then the curtain billowed and shook as something pressed itself against it—the contours of a figure, of a mouth gaping open—

I wheeled around and ran.

I passed other rooms, flashing by in my vision. Radio static spilled from one, piercing the silence. Frantic whispering came from another. The same several syllables, over and over, in a strange language I didn't recognize. A bright light twinkled in another, halfway obscured by a shadow. I kept running, my feet slipping underneath me.

Almost there. I could see the end of the hallway now. The door for the stairwell.

There was just one problem.

Between me and the stairs, there was a door swinging open. Creaking loudly on its hinges. I burst into a sprint and kept my eyes locked ahead of me, not turning to look into the open room—

I saw it anyway.

There was someone standing inside the room. Just a foot or two within the doorway. It looked like an old man, wearing a faded, stained hospital gown. With long, wild gray hair and sunken, pale skin.

He didn't react as I passed. Just stood absolutely still.

As soon as I passed him, though, I heard the distinct *smack* of bare feet on linoleum.

I leapt for the door. His footsteps grew louder behind me—

And then his hand grabbed mine.

I screamed. I tried to yank my hand back, but his fingers wrapped around mine. Holding me tight in a vice grip. Squeezing so hard my joints cracked as I tried to yank away. He stared at me with ice blue eyes, grinning to bare yellowed, crooked teeth. *No no no—*

I yanked—and my hand finally slipped free.

I sprinted to the stairwell, flung the door open, and ducked inside.

I ran down the stairs, nearly tripping over myself. When I finally opened the door to the first floor, relief flooded me. It was like surfacing above water after nearly drowning. Color and light, all kinds of sounds—murmurs of conversation, monitors beeping, footsteps. I stumbled to the nearest chair and collapsed in it, my heart still pounding.

"Where the hell have you been?" a voice snapped, jerking me out of my thoughts.

I looked up to Dr. Harris leaning over me, his features twisted into a scowl. "Sorry, I—I went to look for Hayley on floor 4... that's where you took her. Isn't it?"

His eyes widened. Dark anger flashed across his face. "You disobeyed me," he said in a low growl. "You'll pay for that."

Then he hurried away.

As I sat there in shock, I noticed that everyone was hurrying around. Nurses, doctors, patients being wheeled around in stretchers. And I remembered what that nurse had told me at the beginning of my shift.

It was the night rush.

I got up and headed towards triage. As I did, I passed the waiting room.

It was packed. Even though it'd been completely empty, not fifteen minutes before. And as the crowd of people passed in my peripheral vision... I saw horrible things. An old woman, leaning out of her chair, with black pits for eyes. A woman screaming at the top of her lungs as she raked her hands across the wall. A middle-aged man lying on the floor, turned away from me, shaking as he sobbed.

I stopped dead in my tracks and turned towards the room. But when I did, everything snapped back to normal. The little old lady patiently sat in her chair, sniffling, waiting to be seen. The woman who'd been screaming paced the room calmly. The middle-aged man scrolled through his phone.

What the hell?

My entire body shook. I forced myself to keep walking, my legs weak underneath me. *I'm so tired. It's been so long since I've had to stay up all night. Maybe I'm dreaming... seeing things. Nothing about this makes sense.*

I took a deep breath, tried to compose myself as best I could, and entered the first triage room. There was a woman who'd been in a car accident. I admitted her for a concussion. Then I moved to the next room; there was an old man with symptoms of a heart attack. I kept going for a half hour or so, rushing from room to room, trying to help the patients as best I could.

Then my pager beeped. I was needed in room 5. Confused, I rushed to the room—and my mouth fell open.

It was my wife. She was lying on the bed, moaning in pain, clutching her belly. Tears running down her cheeks.

"I was fine," she muttered weakly, between contractions. "But then, all of a sudden, the contractions started. Really bad. Nothing and then just... intense, horrible pain."

My mind reeled backwards. Dr. Harris's words echoed in my head: *You'll pay for that.* I shook my head —there's no way he could supernaturally put my wife into premature labor. That was ridiculous.

Right?

Did I fall asleep? Maybe when I was in the on-call

room, I'd fallen asleep. Maybe everything since that point had been a dream. A nightmare. I pinched my arm. Glanced a few times at the clock. But everything pointed at reality. At this all being real.

"Dr. Ramirez."

I was snapped out of my thoughts by the nurse. "She needs an emergency C-section, *now*," she said to me. "Her blood pressure's through the roof. Pre-eclampsia. If we don't act now..."

She didn't need to say the last words. I knew them by heart, ever since she was diagnosed by her doctor.

She'll die.

We wheeled her deeper into the hospital. The OBGYN on staff entered the room, and the blue screen went up. We put on our masks and hairnets and I sucked in a breath, waiting for the doctor to start, holding Catalina's hand tightly.

"It's going to be okay," I whispered to her, stroking her hand.

"I'm so scared," she replied, her voice shaking.

It went by so fast. Within minutes I heard the shrill cry of a newborn filling the room. Then he was placed in my arms. I looked down at his perfect little face, screaming as he took his first breaths, and my heart soared. One of the nurses carefully took him from my arms over to the weighing station and I watched, tears burning at my eyes.

I was so enamored with him, I almost didn't hear Dr. Harris come in. And his voice behind me, low and soft: "Transfer her to floor 4."

My heart stopped.

Dr. Harris shoved past me and grabbed the sides of the gurney, then wheeled her out of the room towards the elevator. "Hey! Stop! Where are you taking her?!"

I ran after him. But as I did, I realized how pale Catalina looked. Ashen gray. Her eyes were open, but they weren't blinking, weren't moving. She was just staring at the ceiling. Focusing on nothing.

No. No, no, no...

I squeezed into the elevator just as it began to close. The elevator thrummed underneath us, taking us up to floor 4.

"What are you doing?" I shouted at Dr. Harris.

"Dr. Ramirez," he said calmly, "a life must be given for a life. It's just the order of things. There is an old man in room 4, in cardiac arrest. He will die... unless someone else dies in his place."

"You're going to let my wife die?" I choked out. "So he can live?"

"The old man is wealthy. *Immensely* wealthy. He can pay more. This hospital isn't cheap to run, you know." He glanced at me with a grin. "Besides, you actively disobeyed my orders."

"You can't do that!"

"I've done it before. Hundreds of times. To people like Hayley Johnson," he said, and he smiled crookedly. "The spirits get restless sometimes, and come back down here around midnight. Wander the halls. Wait in the emergency room. Looking for revenge, for closure, for something. We just send them back up to their resting place. Ah, look—here we are."

Ding.

The doors rolled open.

The floor was no longer dark. Lights flickered overhead, lending a strange, strobe-light effect in the abandoned hospital wing. I stepped out onto the floor.

All the doors were open now.

And in the rooms... Someone sat in each one, on a hospital bed. But they weren't injured, or in pain; they were calm. Sleeping, reading, staring at the blue glow of an unseen television.

And in one of the rooms closest to the elevator, I saw a woman inside that looked familiar.

Hayley Johnson.

"It's time," Dr. Harris said, as he began to roll the gurney out of the elevator.

And that's when I saw it. Ahead of us, someone was standing in the middle of the hallway. My heart leapt into my throat.

It was the man in the hospital gown.

He slowly stalked down the dark hallway, smiling. In his hand was a long, curved blade that glimmered in the blinking lights—a scythe. His wild gray hair fell over his face, casting long shadows over his sunken skin. His gaunt face resembled a skull in the dim light, his eyes black pits that went on forever.

No.

I grabbed Dr. Harris by the shoulders and threw him to the ground. Then I yanked the gurney back into the elevator. I jammed my thumb against the 'close door' button. For a heart-stopping moment, nothing happened.

Then, with a shrill squeak, the doors began to close.

Dr. Harris was scrambling up, his face twisted in anger. I darted forward, putting myself between Catalina and them, praying the doors would shut—

Thump.

The elevator began to descend.

When the doors opened again, I rolled Catalina back out onto the first floor. Her eyes jittered for a second, then focused on me. "Where... where am I?" she asked.

"It doesn't matter," I whispered back. "All that matters is that you're alive."

The next few months went by in a blur, as we adjusted to life as new parents. Our son has been nothing but a complete joy. Well, okay, the nighttime wakeups aren't my favorite. But every day, I'm thankful that all three of us are here. That my wife didn't die during childbirth. That I was able to pull her back from Floor 4.

I quit my job at Elmdale Memorial Hospital, and we moved a few hundred miles away, out into the country. And things are happy. Wonderful.

But every so often, when I wake up in the middle of the night, I see a bit of movement in the corner of my eye. Out the window, up on the hill behind our house.

It looks like an old man in a tattered hospital gown.

Holding a scythe.

A PHONE CALL WITH MY HUSBAND

"How are you doing?"

My heart melts when I hear his voice. "I'm doing okay," I say. I can't help but smile.

"How are the kids?"

"They miss you." I bring the phone into the playroom. "Hey, Isabelle, Jackson! Say hi to Daddy!"

Isabelle smiles and leans into the phone. "Hi, Daddy," she says. At only four, she's already such a wonderful little sweetheart.

But when I bring the phone to Jackson, his face goes cold. He shakes his head furiously. "No."

"Why not?"

He pauses, glaring at me. "That's not my *real* daddy."

"Jackson!"

"It's not! *It's not!*" he screams. He shakes his head wildly, stomping on the ground. *"It's not my daddy!"*

I pull the phone away, on the verge of tears. "I'm sorry. He's been acting up lately... I can't—"

"It's okay. I understand." A laugh comes through the other line, cut with a bit of static. "I was like that too when I was four."

"Six," I correct him. "Jackson is six."

A pause.

"I miss you so much," I tell him.

"I miss you, too."

I want to tell him more. So much more. But there isn't much time. I pull it away from my ear and stare at the screen. 1 minute, 17 seconds remaining.

So I ask him to tell me about our first date. At that Italian restaurant on the lake. It sounds exactly like the way he used to tell it to our friends. All the laughs timed at the right places. When I spilled the glass of wine on myself. When we ran out into the pouring rain.

And then, after he's done, I hear the dreaded *beep*.

I whisper goodbye and pull the phone away from my ear.

Your call with MemorialAI has ended.

Pay $99.99 $59.99 for five more minutes!

I glance up at the mantel. The photos of us. Smiling, beaming, arms around each other. And in the center: a cold, stone-gray urn.

I'm lucky that Daniel posted so much of his life online. I always complained about his time on Facebook, and Instagram, and all his 'vlogging' attempts on YouTube. But now—now that I can hear his voice, *talk* to him, 2 years after his death—I'm eternally thankful. Because without all that material, the AI wouldn't have much to train itself on.

I wipe my eyes.

Then I click the button for five more minutes.

I LET SOMETHING INTO MY HOUSE

I've lived in this house for almost a decade. We've never had the slightest hint of paranormal activity. No phantom footsteps, no slamming doors, no shadow people. Nothing.

Until yesterday.

I'd had a weird day. I'm psychologist, and I had a somewhat stressful session with a teenage girl. Obviously can't get into specifics because of privacy and all that, but it was stressful. I didn't think anything of it at the time, but on my way home, I kept glancing in my rearview mirror. It was just instinct—there was no one tailgating me, flashing their highbeams, or anything. In fact, I was alone on the winding country road that led up to my house.

I just kept glancing in the rearview mirror, without even thinking about it.

When I got home, the house was chaos, as usual. Our daughter was running around with stickers, putting them on everything. My poor husband was hopelessly unsticking each one, at about half the speed she was putting them on.

"Need help?" I asked.

"No, but could you make some chicken nuggets?"

I walked over to the fridge—and that's when I saw it.

There was a dirty handprint on the freezer door.

But the problem was, the hand was small—yet, too high up to be my kids'. I stared at it for a second, confused.

I guess Seth was carrying her, and she touched the fridge.

I grabbed the dishtowel and rubbed it off.

We got Lily into bed around eight. I was nearly falling asleep as I read her a story—as I said, it'd been a hard day. My words drawled as I read *Goodnight Moon* for the zillionth time. My arm felt like lead on the pillow.

But then Lily said something that woke me right up.

"Mommy," she said, "who's the girl in the fireplace?"

I looked down at her. "Huh?"

"The girl in the fireplace," she repeated, indignant. "Who *is* she?"

My throat went dry. "There's no girl in the fireplace."

"There *is!*" she insisted. "The girl with no face. She was sitting in the fireplace."

"Okay, let's go to bed," I said, though my heart was pounding. "Time to sleep."

After she fell asleep, I asked Seth about it. "Didn't say anything to me about it," he said. "But that's creepy as fuck."

"I know."

I wanted to just go to sleep and forget about it. But eventually, my anxiety got the better of me. *Sometimes we leave the door unlocked. Sometimes Sammie—the girl a few doors down—comes over unannounced to play with Lily.*

What if she got stuck in the fireplace or something?

What if she's asphyxiating in there right now?

The logical part of my brain knew that was ridiculous. I would've seen police cars outside their house. Tanya would have called me, to see if Sammie was over here. There would have to be like, five super-unlikely things that would all have to happen for Sammie to be trapped in our fireplace, dying.

Still. I had to go check.

"I'm just going to check the fireplace," I said, starting for the door.

Seth laughed. "She scared you."

"Just... I'll be right back."

I'm sure it's nothing. Lily says weird shit all the time. I walked downstairs and turned left, into the darkened family room.

I reached for the switch and flicked on the light.

Just in time to see thin strands of long, black hair retract into the chimney.

I froze. My skin prickled. I couldn't move as I

stared at the fireplace, the place where I'd just seen —*no, could it really be? That would mean someone was inside the chimney, hanging upside-down—*

I finally sucked in a breath.

"SETH!"

He shot down the stairs. "What's wrong?" he asked as he ran into the room.

"Someone's in the chimney—*I saw their hair—*"

Seth frowned. I could tell he didn't really believe me. "Okay," he said slowly, calmly. He approached the fireplace. "Hello?"

Nothing.

He paused for a second. Then he grabbed the fire poker and got on his hands and knees. Gripping the poker in one hand, and his phone with the flashlight on in the other, he slowly pushed his head into the fireplace.

And looked up.

"There's nothing there," he said. "The flue's open, though. So good thing we checked." He pulled his head back out and closed the flue. It clanged shut.

"I didn't open the flue," I said.

"Neither did I. I guess we left it open after the last time we lit a fire which was... shit... like two weeks ago. Man, that's probably like fifty bucks of heat we've been paying for."

He started for the stairs.

"Are you sure there was nothing there?"

"Absolutely positive," he replied.

I swallowed. *Had I imagined it?* As a psychologist, I knew the brain is a funny thing. A bit of hair or dust in our peripheral vision can seem like a face or a shadow person to our brain. Our brains are programmed to recognize faces, humans, danger. Like seeing faces in patterns—pareidolia.

I got on my hands and knees and looked up into the chimney, just to make sure the flue was closed. Then I headed back upstairs.

Something woke me up in the middle of the night.

I rolled over and looked at the clock. 3:07 AM. I closed my eyes and tried to fall back asleep.

But then I heard it.

Clang!

A muffled, metallic clang. Coming from inside the house.

Clang!

I shook Seth awake. As he was getting his bearings, I ran over to Lily's room. Relief flooded me as I saw her fast asleep in bed.

Seth stumbled into the hallway. "What is that?" he whispered.

"I don't know—should I—should I call the police?"

Clang!

This sound was louder than the others. And then—

THUMP.

Coming from our family room.

Seth ran down the stairs. I heard his footsteps

recede into the family room, and for an agonizing moment, there was silence.

Then he shouted:

"Call the police! *Now!*"

When the police arrived, I realized why he was so panicked.

There were sooty footprints on our family room floor.

Bare feet. Small, like those of a child. They wound in a sinusoidal pattern, until fading and disappearing when they got halfway across the room.

There were no footprints leading back.

And the flue was open again.

I don't know what to do. The police didn't find evidence of anything. They insist the footprints must've been caused by Lily. I know they weren't. She was fast asleep. And she told me she didn't make them.

And I keep thinking back to that stressful session I had with that teenage girl. During the session, she was upset—and she grabbed my hand. A little weird and boundary crossing, but she was crying, and desperate for comfort.

When she finally removed her hand, there was this blackish, sooty smudge on my hand. I'd figured it was just some eyeliner or mascara or something. Even though she looked like she wasn't wearing any.

Now, I'm not so sure.

This morning, I dialed her number to schedule her next appointment—and all I got was a robotic voice telling me the number had been disconnected.

THIS IS MY HOUSE

I've lived here for thirty years.

Even if I wanted to leave, I couldn't. My very life is suffused into these halls. The pencil marks behind the closet door, marking my children's growth. Johnny's baby tooth—we never found it, so it's still here, somewhere, in a crag between the floorboards or a dusty, forgotten corner. There's still the echo of a stain on the carpet—once a deep blood-red, now faded to a creamy pink.

Our skin still sits in the vents, our hair still coils deep in the drain.

No one could ever truly scrub this place of our presence.

But you tried. After you and Adam moved in, you tried to bleach and paint and scrub my existence away. But you failed. The markings are still here, in the closet, even if they're under a layer of *Eggshell White*. Nobody found Johnny's little tooth. You ripped up the carpet, but the stain is still there, on the floorboards underneath. A deep rusty red.

You gave a little gasp when you saw it. I enjoyed that.

You thought this was *your* house now, because what? You'd purchased it according to the laws of men? A monetary transaction? Who, or what, *owns* a place has nothing to do with money. There is so much underneath the surface of mortal existence, so many laws and rules that us as humans aren't equipped to understand.

I remember that fateful night, only a few weeks after you moved in. February 24th. When you tried to get rid of me for good. You thought, after everything that happened, this house was finally yours. You were wrong.

"Leave!" you screamed in my face. *"This is my house now!"*

I just smiled.

"It's mine!"

I smiled wider.

You sulked for a while. Kept yourself in the attic, where even I didn't care to go. Only bats and dust up there, and that dingy little window. You can have that part of the house, honey, if you really want.

From that dingy window, you probably watched the new couple move in. They're cute, aren't they? A pregnant white woman with a button nose, and a man with brown skin and a beautiful smile. They, too, will try to scrub this house of my existence. And yours, now.

I don't think the realtor told them why the house went back on the market so quickly.

I don't think she told them that Adam murdered you on the night of February 24th, only three weeks ago.

But no matter how hard they try, this house will never be theirs. And it will never be yours, either.

Because you may have died here—

But I *lived* here.

And there's only room for one fucking ghost.

I HEAR SOMEONE WALKING BESIDE ME EVERY NIGHT

I first heard it a week ago.

I was driving down a side street with the windows open. As I came up to the stop sign, I heard a sound from my right: *tap-tap-tap-tap*.

It sounded like footsteps.

I looked around. No one was on the sidewalk. At least not that I could see, from the light of my headlights. As I slowed for the stop sign, the *taps* decreased in frequency. Like they were slowing down with me.

When I came to a stop, the sound stopped. When I pulled out, it started again.

Must be something with the car. Something with the motor or the muffler or something.

But then, two days later when I went for a jog, I heard it. A distinct *slap-slap-slap* sound, coming from behind me.

At first, I thought it was just the beat of *Journey*

through my earbuds. But when I yanked one out, I still heard it. *Slap-slap-slap.*

Coming from right behind me.

I glanced behind me. No one was there.

I stopped and wheeled around, looking for anything out of place. The footsteps stopped too.

I turned around and started jogging towards my car. The footsteps started back up. I broke into a sprint. The footsteps sped up with me.

I raced to my car and dove inside. After I was safely locked inside, I looked around. No one was there.

I stopped going for night runs after that.

My husband Dave agreed that it was weird. But he thought it must just be some random sound—maybe an animal or a structure settling or some machinery somewhere. He had a point, since where I was jogging wasn't too far from where I'd been driving when I first heard the sound.

It was possible there was something off Main Street, a machine or generator or bird or animal, that was making the noise.

It didn't explain why the sound kept time with me, but I tried to brush that under the rug in favor of a reasonable explanation.

But then, I heard it *in our house.*

Dave was at work. I work from home, so I was home alone. I was carrying a load of clean laundry upstairs when I heard it.

Thump. Thump. Thump.

It sounded like someone was climbing the stairs, just a few stairs below me.

I whirled around. No one was there. My heart began to pound. *Just the house settling,* I told myself, as I stood there frozen on the stairs.

I took another step up—

Thump.

I slowly glanced over my shoulder. Nothing. Took another step.

Thump.

I raced up the remaining stairs—

Thumpthumpthumpthump—

I made it to the top. I wheeled around and stared down at the stairs, panting, my heart pounding in my chest.

Nothing there.

I felt dizzy. Weak. Faint. I set the laundry down in the hallway and sat down on the bed. Then I lay down, pulling the covers up over me.

There's nothing there.

I closed my eyes.

Nothing there.

I sighed. Pulled the blanket up to my neck. Adjusted the pillow. Rolled over to get comfortable—

No.

There was a rustling sound. Just like the one I had made—but a second delayed.

Coming from under the bed.

I lay there, my heart pounding, straining to listen for the slightest sound.

Nothing.

Arms shaking, I slowly pushed myself up from the bed.

Rustle.

I stopped. Froze in place. Stayed absolutely still. The seconds stretched into minutes as I forced myself to breathe slowly, to stay calm.

No one's there. It's just your imagination.

I steeled myself, staring at the door. Then, in one fluid motion, I swung my socked feet over the edge of the bed. Stood up. Sprinted to the door.

Thumpthumpthump—

I swung the door open and slammed it shut. I backed away, my ragged breathing echoing through the hallway. "It's all in your head," I whispered to myself. "It's all in your head. It's all in your—"

THUMP.

Something collided with the door. *Hard.*

I backed away, whimpering. Hand clasped over my mouth. *It can't be. It can't be.* The words popped in my head, whispered hushed in my mother's voice, like she'd whispered them so many years ago. I thought it had only been a fairy tale. A way to scare us into being good.

If you do something bad, she'd whispered,
It will follow you around like a shadow.
It will terrorize you relentlessly.
You will never be free.

I backed away from the door, tears filling my eyes. *Thump, thump, thump.* I heard the muffled footsteps from inside the bedroom, mimicking my own.

Then it happened.

My foot landed on the first stair.

For a second, I lost my balance. My arms pinwheeled; I was freefalling, backwards, into the air. As the world spun and blurred around me, I saw something. A dark figure, standing at the top of the stairs. A silhouette.

My hand shot out and locked on the banister. When I looked up, it was gone.

I don't know how long I stood there. Terrified to move. Terrified to take a step, and hear a *thump* behind me, as *it* followed me down the stairs.

The doorbell jerked me out of my thoughts.

I ran down the stairs. Footsteps pounded behind me, out of sync with my own. I swung the door open to find him there.

My neighbor, Brian.

He shot me a wolfish smile. "Hey, sexy—"

I slammed the door in his face.

Then I collapsed onto the floor, crying. Terrified to move.

Terrified to make a sound.

MY DAUGHTER

"Mommy, why don't I look like you?"

I'd been anticipating this question for a while now. It was inevitable. Sooner or later, Emma was going to notice that she didn't look anything like me. At all.

I just didn't realize it would be so soon.

"Sometimes kids don't look like their mommies and daddies," I started. But where could I go from there? Just launch right into it? It'd be a shock to her, no doubt. She might even cry. "That's just the way it is, Emma."

"But all my friends look like their mommies and daddies."

"Well, that's often how it is. But not always."

"My friends are saying things. About how I look." She pouted. "They make me sad."

How do you tell your child that the world is a cruel place? That you will always be judged by your appearance? That you think it'll all go away once you grow up, but really, a lot of adults are just like schoolyard bullies? Finding anyone who's different, and picking them apart, until they can't be put back together again?

"There's nothing wrong with you, sweetheart."

"But why don't I look like you? Why do I look so… different? My friends think it's weird."

I let out a shaky sigh. *Here goes.* "Well, you were adopted, sweetheart. That means that I'm not related to you. But that doesn't make me any less your mother."

She stared at me for a second, with her dark eyes. My heart pounded in my chest as I waited for tears or screams or tantrums. But instead, she just leaned forward and hugged me.

Tears welled in my eyes. "I love you, Emma."

"I love you too."

She pulled away and I looked down at her proudly. *My daughter.* The one with the pale skin, almost bluish in the florescent light. The long dark hair that often fell over her face. Gaunt cheeks and a pointed chin, pitch black irises that matched her pupils.

I still remember that night. When Special X invaded her home. No one stopped to ask questions during the extermination. No one considered that maybe the human male found with her had died of natural causes. No one looked past the long black hair covering her monstrous features, the unnaturally long limbs, the pale blue-gray skin, the pitch-black eyes.

And nobody heard the baby crying in its bedroom, crying for its mother.

Except me.

It's a miracle no one looked closely at the wad of blankets in my arms, as I rushed to my car and drove into the night.

Maybe someday I'll tell her the truth. The whole truth. That she is not a monster. That the only monsters are the men who invaded her home.

But for now, she is my little girl.

And that is enough.

A PYRAMID SCHEME FOR THE DARK LORD

My heart sunk as soon as I saw the message.

Hey hun!! Long time no talk! How are you? 👻

I have a question 🐚 **for you** 👓 **How would you like to retire by 30?!** ✋ **I just started with this new boss** 🏰 **and it's an AMAZING source of income!!** 💩 **I could get you in on it!** 🤪🤪🤪

I hadn't talked to Kelly since high school, and even then, she was a royal bitch to me. We mostly ran in different circles, but she never passed up a good opportunity to get a zinger in about my weight.

And now she was trying to rope me in to her multi-level-marketing / pyramid scheme?

Oooh, I could have fun with this.

Hey Kelly! I began to type. **How are you girl?!** 😍😍😍 **I'm so glad you contacted me! I was JUST thinking of contacting you because ...**

I paused at the keyboard, thinking through my options.

I'm writing a book on how to eliminate feminine odor!! I thought you'd be the PERFECT reader, given your history!

Stifling giggles, I hit send.

Okay. I have to admit, that was pretty immature. I'm almost thirty. I should have more class. But, man, did it feel *good*.

I got up and poured myself a glass of wine, not expecting her to reply. But when I got back to the keyboard, there was an answer.

Sure I'll read your book! I'm sure it's great 😊 But would you like to hear 🙂 about working for me? 💰 💼 💰 I swear you won't regret it!!

My smile faded a little. Wow—she must really be desperate for money. I navigated to her profile on Facebook while the Messenger chat window was still open, and clicked on her profile picture.

She looked different. Older, of course, but also... worn down. She wasn't wearing makeup—in high school, she wore so much she could be a Kardashian—and deep bags sat under her eyes. I noticed that her profile no longer listed a relationship status. *Did Brian leave her?*

I couldn't help it. I'm a very sympathetic person. Even though this girl was super mean to me in high school, I felt bad. She looked like a shell of her old self in those photos. Maybe it wasn't her fault—maybe she'd gotten hit with cancer or illness. Maybe Brian turned out to be a cheating scumbag.

Maybe this was her, earnestly, trying to pick herself back up.

Ok, I definitely don't want to work for you, sorry. I'm all too familiar with pyramid / MLM schemes. But if you have any products you're selling, I'll take a look.

Against my better judgement, I hit send. It wouldn't kill me to buy something... well, actually, given the class-action lawsuits against quite a few MLMs, maybe it would. Still. I'd be willing to throw in $10 for some shitty product if it would help her. She really did look terrible.

I watched as three little dots appeared. She was typing.

It's barely work, it's fun! 😜😜😜 **And you'll get so much money!** 🤑 💰 **So what do ya say?? YES??** 🙏

Okay. My sympathy was gone. I'd extended a hand and she was just tromping all over it. **Sorry. I'm not interested**, I wrote back.

I leaned back and took a long sip of wine. But no familiar *pings* sounded from my computer; she wasn't chatting back. That surprised me. Was it really that easy? Just say no and they're gone? Man, I'd have to remember that for next—

Tap-tap-tap.

Three short knocks at my front door.

I jumped and nearly sloshed wine all over myself. Setting down the glass, I slowly pulled myself up on the sofa, staring at the front door. *It's almost 10—who'd be coming by this late?*

Ping.

I glanced at my computer—to see a new message from Kelly.

Three words that made my blood run cold.

Answer the door.

I glanced at the door. Then back at the chat screen. I grabbed my phone and darted into the hallway, then backed into my bedroom and locked the door.

Shit kelly, are you outside my front door right now?!

Three dots. And then the response:

Answer the door.

No. It can't be her. She has no idea where I live. I swallowed and looked down at the phone. This was too far. I hadn't seen Kelly in more than a decade. The last I heard, she'd still lived in our hometown, over a hundred miles away.

This is insane.

What tf is wrong with you?!, I typed, my thumbs racing across the screen. **You can't just come to my house! Get OUT of here, NOW!!** I crept over to the window and parted the blinds, peering outside. I couldn't see the entire porch from this angle, but I could see the steps and the sidewalk.

And the long shadow falling over them, cast by the porchlight.

She was still there.

Ping. I looked down to see the same three words. **Answer the door.**

Go away NOW, I wrote back, my thumbs slipping over the screen. **Please.**

Tap-tap-tap. Ping. **Answer the door.**

I sucked in a breath, my hands shaking. I'd seen a

car parked further up my street when I got back from work. Was that her?! Had she been stalking me all day? And why me? I hadn't seen her in so long. She was the bully—I never wronged her. There were dozens of people who'd crossed her in high school, and I wasn't one of them. I mainly ignored her and took out my anger on video games and bad goth poetry.

I swear, if you're not gone in five minutes I'm calling the cops, I wrote back. **And my boyfriend is super pissed and will chase you out of here personally if the cops don't come in time,** I added.

If she was watching me, she probably knew that was a lie. But whatever. Hopefully it would scare her enough to leave.

Three dots appeared on the screen.

And then they disappeared.

I peered through the blinds and watched as the shadow shifted. *She's leaving. Thank God.* I let out a shaking breath, lowering my phone—

I froze.

The person leaving my porch wasn't Kelly.

It was a man, tall and broad, wearing dark clothing. A hoodie, pulled tight over his head. A white plastic mask.

A baseball bat hung from his hand.

But he didn't walk towards the street. Instead, he began walking around the side of the house. I held my breath as he disappeared around the corner.

Fuckfuckfuck. He's going to break in.

I immediately swiped out of messenger and called 911.

Thirty seconds later, I was assured by the operator that the police were on their way. But they were ten, maybe fifteen, minutes out. With shaking hands, I swiped back over to the chat window.

There was a new message from Kelly.

If you do not answer the door, we will come in by force.

THE POLICE ARE ON THEIR WAY, I typed back. **AND MY BOYFRIEND'S GETTING HIS SHOTGUN FROM THE CLOSET.**

Three dots. And then the heart-stopping reply:

You don't have a boyfriend.

No, no, no. I ran into the closet and pulled the doors over me. **WHAT DO YOU WANT??** I typed. **WHY ARE YOU DOING THIS??**

The response came quickly.

The Dark Lord needs the blood of a virgin.

And we all know you're too fat to get laid.

What the fuck? So Kelly had gone insane. Like, batshit insane. And now she had... what... hired her boyfriend to break into my house and get my blood? For some cult or imaginary dark lord?

Another message popped up.

If you just agreed to join, we could've done this the easy way.

And then, an instant later—the sound of breaking glass.

My entire body froze. I held my breath. The closet was too warm. Suffocating. **Please, just tell him to**

go, I typed back. **If you just get him to leave, I won't tell the police. And my blood won't even work, because I'm not a virgin. So please, just stop this. This is crazy. Do you really want to go to jail? You or your boyfriend?**

Three dots appeared.

Footsteps sounded inside the house. Getting louder.

But then, another sound. Sirens, in the distance. Growing louder.

The dots disappeared.

I didn't move until the police were shouting through the door, asking me to open up. I would've just stayed in the closet until they actually lifted me to safety, but I didn't want them to break down the door —I was too broke to replace it. So I crept out into the hallway and then sprinted for my life to the door.

The police took fingerprints and studied the evidence, but the man seemed to be wearing gloves. None of the evidence led them to a suspect.

I handed over the messages from Kelly, but by the time the police got there, she'd fled. She's probably somewhere across the country by now, changing her name, trying to find a new victim.

Or, maybe she'll keep coming after me.

Because I received one final message from Kelly's Facebook account, before it was deactivated. Four words. Plus an emoji.

Catch ya later, hun 😏

THE LAKE IS NOT WET

The lake is not wet. It is not made of water. I kneel at the shoreline, slipping my hand into its depths. But when it comes out, it is dry.

It feels warm. Warmer than water should be. And there is a strange stillness to it. I do not feel any currents—even though it's quite windy here. There are no ripples, no disturbances, no movement.

The lake is completely, utterly still.

There's something off about the reflections on the lake, too. Even though the sky is nearly dark, there's a sort of brightness to it. Like it's emitting its own light. The water sparkles and reflects the deep green trees, swaying in the wind.

I'm cold. It got darker earlier than I thought it would. The water's warmth is so tantalizing in this cold, dark place. I raise my hand to dip them in again —and in the dying light, I realize something is wrong with my hands. They're all pruny, like they've been in the water for hours. But they're not even wet. There is no slick layer of water on my skin. My hands don't shine and glint and drip. They are dry. They must be.

But I need to feel the warmth.

I plunge my hands in.

I stare at the boundary between my arms and the not-water. The water dips in slightly where it meets my skin. Like I've just pushed my arms into an enormous vat of gelatin. It occurs to me that maybe there's a microscopic layer of air, between my skin and this material. Maybe that's why my skin isn't wet. I plunge my arms in further, almost up to my elbows, but I can't feel the bottom.

I stand up, unfold myself, and dip my foot in. I still can't feel the bottom. But I need the warmth. I need to feel it. So I keep lowering my foot, lower and lower—

A hand shoots out from the depths and grabs me by the ankle. I kick and scream, but it's tightened around me like a vice grip. And it's pulling me—oh God, it's pulling me down—

I open my mouth to scream, but my lungs are full of water.

And then I plunge into the depths of the lake.

July 23, 2023

PIEDMONT, PA – The body of a young woman was found washed up on the shoreline of Lake Piedmont. Dental records have revealed her to be Mara Johnson, 21, who went missing two weeks ago.

Witnesses reported seeing "human hands" poking out of the lake's surface. The lifeguard, believing it to be someone drowning, swam in after her and grabbed her by the ankle, pulling her to shore. Only then did he realize the woman had already passed away, long before.

Anyone with information on Mara Johnson's disappearance should contact the Piedmont Police Department at XXX-XXX-XXXX.

I HEAR VOICES

"I hear voices. But I'm not crazy."

Dr. Kowalski gave me an understanding smile. But I knew what he was thinking. *That's what they all say.* Hearing voices, insisting you're not crazy—it's like the textbook definition of being crazy.

"When I hear the faucet running, or water gurgling down the drain—I hear things. Words. But I think it's just my brain, trying to make sense of the random noises I'm hearing."

"So, like pareidolia," he replied.

"Pareidolia?"

"When you see a pattern in wood, or a stain on a rug, and it looks like a face. But this is auditory pareidolia—you're hearing random patterns, and your brain is trying to make sense of it."

"I guess so. But... it's gotten worse." I started to fidget. "At first, I would just hear random things. The water going down the drain sounded like it was saying 'GLOW.' When I made the bed, the rustle of the blankets sounded like someone whispering 'SNAKE.' Just really random, stupid stuff."

He nodded, but I could tell I was losing him. He didn't like where this was going.

"Then, I started to hear things that made more sense. The worst was with Orson's white noise machine. It's a crappy one, and it plays the same five-second clip of 'babbling brook' on loop. As I'm trying to fall asleep, my brain picks up all these repeating patterns. And then, just when I think I might actually fall asleep... I start to hear the words."

Dr. Kowalski rubbed his temples.

"It's always the same words. Even when he changes the sound, it's the same words."

"And what are those words, Darla?"

I swallowed.

"'HELP ME.'"

Dr. Kowalski sighed. A heaving, disappointed sigh.

He thought I was crazy.

I didn't really blame him. Now that I was hearing myself say it out loud, it did sound a little crazy. Maybe Orson was right. Maybe I did need this appointment. If he hadn't made it for me, I never would've gotten around to it... and maybe things would've spiraled out of control.

"Listen. I know it sounds crazy. But if I were crazy, wouldn't I be hearing the voices when it's totally quiet, too?"

"Not necessarily."

I stared at the wall, chewing my lip.

"I'm going to prescribe you an antipsychotic. A low dosage. We'll try it, see if it helps."

My heart plummeted. All the air sucked out of my lungs.

"Okay," I finally choked.

We talked a little more, I thanked him, and he gave me my prescription. I couldn't leave the office fast enough. But then, halfway to my car, I realized—I'd left my phone in the office.

I went back in. But as I reached for the doorknob, I stopped dead.

"I just saw her, Orson," I heard Dr. Kowalski say from the other side of the door.

My husband's name.

"You're going to have to get a better white noise machine."

...What?

"Darla can hear her."

THE ZMORY

There was a strand of flesh hanging from my bedroom door.

It was lit by the moonlight, streaming in through my window. Pale and ghastly with a slight sheen to it. Dangling from the brass keyhole. It wasn't uniform, but lumpy in spots; thicker at the bottom, where it met the floor.

And it was *growing*.

I lay there in bed, terrified. My brain screaming to move, but all I could do was watch. Watch the flesh accrete on the floor. Slowly pooling out, forming a shape.

The shape of two knobby, twisted feet.

Some of my friends joked that such an old farmhouse might come with some unwanted guests, back when I bought it. I scoffed. "I don't believe in ghosts. All that supernatural stuff is for idiots."

Now I realize, no one believes in ghosts, until they see one.

I replayed the images in my head, of that fleshy strand coming down from the keyhole. *A nightmare. It had to be a nightmare, right?* It didn't even sound like a ghost. It was just... weird. Like all dreams are. Like a Salvador Dali painting on steroids. *And I couldn't move. It was like textbook sleep paralysis.*

As a precaution, I duct-taped shut every single keyhole in the house. Then, after I'd retired to my bedroom for the night, I taped every single crack and cranny in that room. So that it was airtight. The gap under the door. Even the crack between the floorboards.

Just in case.

Of course it wasn't real. But just in case. For peace of mind.

But I forgot the vent.

I woke up with a start.

At first, I thought nothing was wrong. My room was dark and quiet. The keyhole was taped. I was safe.

Then I saw the flesh coming out of the floor.

It had been cut into thick ribbons, like a hock of ham on a deli slicer. Growing upwards from the vent, undulating in the draft. The pieces coalesced midair, and as they did, a naked, dirty bellybutton appeared.

Underneath it, a tangle of gray pubic hair.

No. No. This can't be happening.

This can't be real.

I tried to move—but I was paralyzed.

I watched in horror as the ribbons coalesced further. Into a naked, pale woman standing over my bed.

I couldn't turn my head. But out of the corner of my eye, I could see her face. Gaunt and long. Tangled gray hair. Yellowed, crooked teeth.

Her eyes empty, endless voids.

And then I heard something that turned my blood to ice—the sheets rustling.

Without moving my head, I glanced down—to see her hand sliding over my bedsheets. Pointed fingernails, filthy, coming right for me. Emaciated fingers almost bluish in the darkness.

I opened my mouth to scream, but I couldn't. It was like those nightmares I'd had, even as a kid. Where I open my mouth to scream for help, but only a suffocated squeak comes out.

The hand slid closer.

And then her skin contacted mine.

Something like a *zap,* a tingle of electricity, coursed through my skin. It radiated up my arm, stinging and cold. I think the woman was smiling wider, now, but I couldn't turn my head enough to see her clearly.

And then everything went back.

———————

In the morning I was tired. So incredibly tired. *That must have been a dream,* I kept telling myself. But I knew it wasn't. I could barely walk downstairs to eat breakfast. It was like I was controlling a body double my weight.

I left the house that morning.

Later in the evening, from the comfort of a friend's house, I did some research. I didn't tell Kate what happened; it was too unbelievable. I'd sound crazy. I told her there was a problem with the house (true), and I might be at risk for carbon monoxide poisoning (false.)

But in all my Google searches, something popped up: *zmory*. Polish for 'nightmare.' The name of a creature from old Polish folklore, that steals one's life force. A ghost, sort of, but one that can't pass through walls...

But changes shape, instead.

Like turning into a thin strand, to fit through a keyhole.

I'm never going back there.

I'd sell the house, even though it'd be at a loss. I'd move into an apartment, whatever, any place else. Hell, I'd even take on a roommate. And I *hated* roommates. Even the spouse kind—hence being single at 42.

Kate reassured me I could stay as long as I needed to. That night, I snuggled into bed and pulled the comforter up to my neck, comforted by the warm glow of the nightlight in the hall. It shone through the crack under the door, dimly lighting the entire room.

I closed my eyes and began to sleep—

Smack.

A wet, horrible sound.

When my eyes flew open, I could no longer see the night light's glow.

As my eyes adjusted to the darkness, I saw the pancake of flattened flesh, pulling itself into the room.

No. No—this is a nightmare.

I left!

The woman at my side. Black pits staring down at me. A jolt of electricity through my arm.

When I woke up the next day, I could barely get out of bed. I scrambled for my phone and frantically pulled up more pages on the *zmory*. That's when I realized I missed a bit of text in one of the articles I'd read—

When a zmory finds its host, it latches on.

It follows.

And it doesn't leave until you die.

MINECRAFT

I've been wanting to play Minecraft for months now. My friend, Kenny, knows this—and also knows I'm broke right now.

So he very generously "got" me a copy. How he got it, I did not ask.

So there I was, on Friday night, opening my (probably bootleg) copy after a stressful week. The house was quiet; my boyfriend was out for the night with his buddies. I'd made myself a cup of chamomile tea and was curled up with a blanket, ready to play. I already knew the basic controls: I'd seen way too many videos on Youtube.

I spawned in a field with a few blocky trees. The square sun hovered over the hill in front of me. I started towards it, veering left and right, trying to get a feel for the terrain. Strangely, I didn't see any animals. No pigs, no goats, no chickens.

But I didn't spend too long exploring. I was in Survival mode, and I know you're supposed to make the most of that first day: cut down trees, get some coal and cobblestone, build a shelter to keep you safe at night. I wanted to build a cute little house in the field but ended up running out of time, so I dug a hole into the side of a hill. Stuck a torch on the wall, cut a 1x1 hole for a window, and called it a day.

That's when things got *weird*.

After a few minutes of nighttime, the mobs started spawning. But they weren't any of the normal ones: no zombies, skeleton archers, or creepers.

There was only one mob. A villager-like creature with grayish skin.

The weirdest thing was their eyes. They weren't just a few pixels—they were *detailed*. Circular and bloodshot, with no irises or pupils.

"And they let *kids* play this?" I muttered to myself. "Yeesh. My mom never would've let me play this."

A few of them huddled around my window. Unlike zombies, they made no noise. All night I watched their grayish shoulders flit in and out of view as they bumped into each other, each trying to get a glimpse of me through my little window.

There was something else weird, too. As far as I could tell, the sky had no stars or moon. It was just black, with nothing else.

I hunkered down in my little hidey-hole until the sun had risen. The creepy creatures were nowhere to be seen.

"Well," I said to myself, "I think I'll try mining today, instead."

I made myself a wooden pickaxe, then a stone one. I dug through the soil and rock, deeper and deeper, until I fell into a cave. It was dark. I grabbed one of my seven torches and stuck it to the wall.

Stone, coal, and some white-colored stone. "Cool," I muttered, as I mined some of the coal. Then I went forward into the darkness, stuck another torch onto the wall. On and on until I ran out of torches.

But, aha! Now I had more coal. I quickly made some more torches, and continued.

The cave descended. The floor grew more steep, the steps downwards being two or sometimes even three blocks high. I continued, though, knowing the deeper I was, the more likely I'd find diamonds. Not that I could even mine them with a stone pickaxe. That I knew, from all those videos.

But this cave didn't seem very much like the ones I'd seen in the videos. I thought zombies, and all the scary mobs, lived in the caves. And those ginormous spiders, too. But I'd yet to see another living thing down here.

Deeper I went, and then I did hear something eerie: a sort of deep whooshing sound. I looked all around, looking for the source; but all I saw were my own torches, climbing up into the cave above me.

I continued further into the cave. And further. It was weird—I thought at some point, you hit lava or bedrock, and you can't go any further down. But this cave seemed to go down and down and down, with no signs of stopping.

No signs of diamonds, either.

I stopped on a small stone landing, before the cave continued even more steeply down. Got out my pickaxe. "Seems as good a place as any," I said, as I dug the pickaxe into the rock. I'd seen the videos on diamond mining, on the optimal spacing of tunnels, all of that. And who knows? Maybe I'd get lucky and find some iron along the way. For some reason, the only ore I'd seen yet was coal.

I watched the cracks appear on the stone block. "Stupid stone pickaxe," I muttered. It finally broke, and then I started on the next one. I only got several blocks in before—*clink!*—my pickaxe broke.

"Daaaammit," I said to myself, heaving a sigh. I turned around, to make a crafting block—

And froze.

There, at the entrance to my tunnel, stood one of the gray creatures.

It stared at me with those white, bloodshot eyes. So perfectly detailed compared to the rest of its pixelated body. It didn't move, didn't advance towards me—just stood there, frozen. Watching me.

"You little fucker."

I switched to the stone sword, started running towards it—

And then I froze again.

Because something caught my eye. Not something in the game. Something here, in real life. *Oh no, no, no—*

The little white light next to my webcam was on.

I snapped the laptop shut. Slid it onto the floor. And then I sat there, panting, my entire body numb. With shaking hands, I picked up my phone.

And sent a text.

Kenny... how exactly did you get Minecraft for me?

MAIL-ORDER HUSBAND

I was on my third glass on wine on a lonely Friday night when I ordered him.

The website seemed fairly innocent—it gave off an old-timey matchmaker vibe, when blind dates were coordinated by people rather than algorithms. *We'll find the perfect man for you. Sign up today to find him!*

I did.

And was more than a bit surprised when a six-foot-long box showed up on my doorstep the next morning.

OPEN IMMEDIATELY, read the warning written on the side in big red letters. And there were holes in the cardboard—several of them, near the top of the box. *Are those... air holes?*

My dog Ruby slunk out of the house behind me. She began sniffing the box like mad, as if there were something *very* interesting inside.

No... there's no way...

I ripped open the box with a pounding heart—

And burst out laughing.

At the bottom of the box was one of those stupid "grow a boyfriend" gag gifts. You know the ones: you put a little plastic man in water, and it grows to several times its size. I'd seen them at my local CVS for Valentine's day.

I'd been pranked.

I picked up the thing. It was a little man about six inches tall, with impressive biceps and pecs, made of a spongy plastic material. All one color—a medium pink-beige. Even his eyes were that color, which was a little creepy.

"Well, aren't you handsome?"

I put him next to my computer. The fact that I'd drunk-bought a plastic boyfriend was actually pretty funny, when you really thought about it.

And a little sad.

I immediately texted my mom and told her I'd meet her friend's son she kept raving about.

―――――――――――

That evening, I ate a steak dinner for one as I continued to work on my proposal. And there sat the plastic, fleshy little man, watching me with his fleshy little eyes.

"What are *you* staring at?"

It stared back with those soulless, beige eyes.

"Yeah, kind of lame that I'm sitting here alone on a Saturday night, huh?" I sighed and glanced over at Ruby. "Look at me. Talking to an inanimate object. I've gone batshit crazy, huh?"

She didn't look up from her chew toy.

Out of sheer boredom, I went into the kitchen and filled a bowl with water. Took him out of his package and plopped him in. But even after a half hour had passed, he only grew about an inch taller.

"Guess you're a shower, not a grower," I said with a snort.

But that night, before I went to bed, I forgot to pour out the water.

I woke up with a start at 4 AM.

It only took me a few seconds to realize what woke me up. There were strange sounds coming from downstairs. A sloshing sound—and then a loud THUMP.

I bolted up in bed.

Someone's in the house.

I'd always had a fear of something like this happening. Masked men breaking into the house in the middle of the night. Killing me in my sleep. I grabbed my phone off the nightstand and clutched it to my chest, straining my ears to listen.

THUMP.

Oh God. He was coming up the stairs.

I threw off the blankets and ran into the closet. Closed the doors and held my breath, watching through the slats as I silently dialed 911.

The door opened.

A man stepped inside. But there was something... *off*... about his movements. Jerky, clumsy, like he didn't quite know how to walk. I held the phone to my ear, whispering my address into the speaker—

His head swiveled towards the closet.

And every muscle in my body froze.

His eyes... they were that awful beige color. Like they were made of skin. As I stared at him, I realized his hair, too—everything—he was beige all over, from his head down to his toes.

A man made entirely of plasticky flesh.

I stifled a scream. Held the phone to my ear, praying he wouldn't come look in the closet...

He stood in the middle of the room, his gaze sweeping over each wall. He paused when his eyes fell on the closet. Slowly, he turned in my direction.

And then he took a step forward.

I held my breath as he took another step. And another. *No no no.* And then he was there—right outside the doors—

He paused.

And leaned forward.

Through the slats I saw him looking at me. Looking at me with those terrible, flesh-covered eyes. Thin veins spiderwebbed across the skin, across where his pupils should be. But somehow... he could *see* me. I could feel it, feel him staring, waiting—

A siren wailed in the distance.

He turned around and slipped out of the door.

THUMP. THUMP. THUMP.

I heard his footsteps recede down the stairs—and then he was gone.

The police found no trace of the man I'd seen. I told them about my order, and showed them the email confirmation—but when I tried to click on the website, it gave me an error message.

Whoever had sold me that *thing*... had completely vanished.

A few days went by and I thought that was the end of it. I'd even convinced myself that it had been some sort of waking nightmare, and what I'd seen never even happened.

But then I got another package.

This one didn't have an address on it. Whoever dropped it off on my porch had hand-delivered it. And it was small—only about six inches long.

With shaking hands I reached down and picked it up.

The smell hit me like a truck as I brought it up to my face. Slowly, I lifted the lid and peered inside—

It was a heart. It looked like it had been torn out of a small animal. Dark liquid pooled at the corners of the container, and I fought the urge to vomit.

Only then did I notice the trail of large footprints in the snow, leading away from my porch.

I think he's going to keep coming back...
I think he *likes* me.

MY HUSBAND WEARS PEOPLE'S FACES

My husband wears other people's faces.
    I don't think he would've told me. I don't think I would've believed him, even if he did. But fate intervened, and when I swung by the grocery store Tuesday after work, it happened.
    As I loaded my stuff onto the conveyor belt, I heard a wet *splat* behind me.
    "*Fiddlesticks.*"
    Fiddlesticks. That's what my husband Mike always said, instead of cursing. I couldn't help but smile. I turned around to see an old man standing behind me, split-open yogurt on the floor. "I'll help you clean that up," I said, pulling some tissues out of my purse.
    He didn't move to help me. Didn't say thank you. Just stared at me, eyes wide, as if he were afraid.
    I ignored it and crouched down, wiping up the yogurt. When I stood back up, he was gone.

Rude, I thought, glancing around for him. *He just... left? Without even thanking me? Without even taking his groceries?*

The groceries.

My heart did a little flip as I saw what, exactly, was on the conveyor belt.

Nonfat blueberry yogurts. A can of black olives. Cinnamon rice cakes. Old Spice shaving cream.

Alone, they didn't mean anything. But together...

That's exactly what Mike buys.

When I got home, Mike was already waiting for me in the living room, his foot tapping the carpet faster than a jackrabbit getting ready to race.

"Elena," he said, as soon as his eyes met mine.

"What's... what's wrong?" I asked.

"I have something to tell you."

No. Every time I heard those words, it never ended well. *I cheated. I lied.* Mike was the first person I thought I'd never hear those words from, after all the hell I'd been through with my exes.

I guess I was wrong.

"That was me, today. Behind you at the grocery store. I... I was wearing someone else's face."

Silence ticked by.

"You mean... like a mask?"

"Like a mask, yeah. But it's not a mask." His blue eyes locked on mine. "It's real."

"What?" was all I could choke out.

"I worked in a mortuary for several years after high school," he continued. With each sentence he spoke, it got worse, and my heart dropped another inch. "When the family asked for a cremation, or a closed casket burial, I'd steal the face of the deceased. Then I began to wear them. If you store them properly, they don't go bad."

Nausea rolled through me.

"People treated me differently, when I was someone else. They didn't treat me like the kid of Cedar Hill's only single mom. When Harvey Thompson died, I wore his face once before his family announced his death. I got a five-course meal at the local steakhouse, all for free."

Eating with someone else's face...

With someone else's lips...

"You okay? You look a little pale."

"I feel like throwing up."

"I know, I know, it sounds terrible. But once you get used to it, it's not so bad."

A long silence passed between us. I stared at the wall, unable to meet his eyes.

"If you need some space, some time to process, that's fine. I get it. But I think you'll realize it isn't so bad. People have all kinds of secrets... drugs, affairs... of all the secrets I could have, it isn't so bad, is it?"

It isn't so bad?

What... the actual fuck?

I found them.

He kept them in the shed out back. He knew I never checked the shed, because that's where his "workshop" was. Turns out, it was less of a workshop and more of a dressing room.

My heart pounded in my chest as I stared at the wall. *He's a psychopath.* Fear flushed through me as I stared at them—saggy, deflated flesh hanging from pegs on the wall. Mostly belonging to white males, from what I could tell, though a few looked like women, and a few didn't match his skin tone.

They looked remarkably like halloween masks of cheap latex. The eyes, nostrils, and mouths cut out. The hair a little mussed and matted. But the skin was a bit translucent on each of them, and a shade too gray to belong to a living human.

Faces that belonged to real people. Compressed and deformed and sagging under their own weight as they hung there.

I ran out of the shed and promptly threw up all over the grass.

But then I forced myself to go back inside.

Because I'd seen something. I'd... *recognized* something.

I slipped back into the shed. Forced myself to look more closely at the faces, even though it made me retch. That one... in the lower right... with the short blond hair and the hook nose. *No, no, no.*

I recognized it.

It was Jon. My college ex. The guy who'd emotionally manipulated me, all through my fragile young adulthood, making me believe I wasn't pretty enough, wasn't loved. Who told me he loved me just to take it back. Who'd broken me and put me back together, just to break me all over again.

And that one, there. The one with the dark hair and the large eye holes. That was Evan, my boyfriend in my late twenties. The one who cheated on me, in the most devastating way, with my best friend while he was out of town. I'd spent days—no, weeks—crying into my pillow, thinking nothing could possibly hurt more than that. *Nothing*.

I was wrong.

This hurt more.

I stared at the several faces I recognized. All exes. All guys who had hurt me in a devastating, awful, horrible way. The kind of pain that lingered long after they had been gone, like a scar on my soul.

I ran out of the shed. Ran to my car. My hands shook as I fit the key in ignition. Then I peeled out of there.

I drove for hours, not even knowing where I was going—except that it was away from him.

I finally stopped at a hotel five hours from home. I checked into a room, locked the door, and collapsed on the bed.

But I'm not sure I'm safe.

Because, as I was writing this, someone knocked on my door. And when I looked through the peephole, I saw a member of the hotel staff standing on the other side—

With faint lines cut around his eyes, his nostrils, his mouth.

I've locked the deadbolt. He can't get in. But at some point, I'll have to leave this room. Maybe tomorrow morning, maybe a week from now.

And he will be waiting for me.

I'M TRAPPED IN AN INFINITE SUBURB

"I think we're lost."

I edged the car along, looking for Rosebud Lane. But all I saw were rows and rows of the same cookie-cutter suburban house, crammed in next to each other, going on forever. Sighing, I pulled over at the curb. "Can you check the GPS?"

"Sure."

As he pulled out his phone, I stared out the windshield. Even though it was a sunny, beautiful day, the neighborhood was a ghost town. Nobody walking their dog on the sidewalk. No kids playing in the street. I glanced around at the houses, and though it was hard to tell from the reflections on the windows—it looked like the curtains were drawn.

Dave sighed next to me. "I don't think is right."

"What do you mean?"

He handed me the phone. The app showed our

location... in the middle of the woods. I zoomed out a bit, but no suburbs showed up.

"Woah, that's weird." I pulled out my phone, but the same thing happened. Little blue dot in the middle of the woods. The closest road was the two-lane highway we'd pulled off of. "Guess this is a really new development."

Google Maps was almost always accurate, but if the houses had just been built, maybe the software hadn't caught up yet. They certainly looked very new—overlapping gables, big windows with no shutters, all neutral colors. The grass perfect, without muddy tracks from dogs or kids. The white siding so crisp and pristine, it almost glowed. The windows shiny as a mirror.

I hated that sterile, almost uncanny look of new houses. Like they'd just been copied and pasted out of a video game and plopped down in the earth. No personal touches, no wear and tear, no character. Just sterile and empty and perfect.

"Maybe you should call Megan," I said.

Dave glanced at the clock. "I don't want to interrupt the shower."

"Yeah, but we're lost, and the GPS isn't working."

He sighed. "If we don't find it in ten minutes, I'll call her."

That was Dave for you. Always thinking of others. Which was nice, of course, until it got to these kinds of things. He'd rather waste our time, driving around aimlessly, than give Megan a quick call for fear of being rude. It was always like that with him.

But whatever. They say pick your fights, and this wasn't important enough to go to battle over.

I continued crawling down the street, past more and more identical houses. But just as I was thinking maybe I *should* force him to call Megan, that this was a fight worth choosing—I saw it.

A turn up ahead.

I sped towards the intersection. Hoping the little green sign said Rosebud Lane. But as we got closer, my stomach dropped.

"What... the hell?"

It was blank.

It was just a green rectangle of metal. No text on it whatsoever.

"Wow, someone fucked up," Dave laughed. "They had *one job...*"

"Do you think I should turn?"

"Wait. Lemme pull up the GPS." The car idled on the corner as I waited for Dave to pull out his phone. "Nah, still in the woods. I guess turn on it, yeah."

I flicked on my blinker and turned onto the unnamed street.

More cookie-cutter houses with curtained windows. All painted a perfectly neutral beige with white trim. Even the front lawns looked identical: three shrubs along the porch, and a big hydrangea on the garage end.

There were no cars in any driveways, either. Just like the previous street. *I wonder if they're so new, some of them haven't even been moved into. Just standing empty.* For some reason, the thought sent a chill down my spine. How weird would it be to live in this neighborhood, surrounded by empty houses?

"I'd hate to live here," I muttered.

"It'd be nice to have something brand-new, though. Not having everything break all the time."

"But every single house looks *exactly* the same." I shook my head. "I bet they have a super strict HOA."

"Probably."

We continued up the road. It seemed like the houses stretched into infinity, disappearing into the light fog. "What was it, again? Number 52?"

"Yep."

I slowed the car, looking for mailboxes, so I could check the house numbers. But the houses didn't have mailboxes. *I guess they must have one of those communal ones,* I thought, *like apartments and townhouses have.* But the houses didn't have numbers on the front doors, or the porches, either.

So weird...

We continued driving, but I couldn't shake the uneasy feeling. Identical houses, extending to infinity. Like someone had just copy-pasted them on a computer screen. I let out a sigh and stared out at the road, looking for signs of life, individuality, anything.

And then, finally—through the gloom and mist—I saw a smudge of color.

A stop sign.

"Oh, good. We'll see what street we're on," I said.

But as we approached, my stomach twisted. My heart pounded in my chest.

There wasn't an intersection.

Or even a crosswalk.

There was no actual reason for cars to stop.

Yet, the stop sign was still there. And there was another one, on the other side of the road, telling cars in the oncoming direction to stop too.

"There's... no reason for a stop sign to be here."

"Maybe it's like an accessibility thing? Like, the person who owns that house is blind. So everyone needs to stop here so they don't hit them?"

"Does that kind of thing even exist? I mean, great if it does, but I've never seen that."

He shrugged.

"I think we should turn around."

"Let's just continue a little bit," Dave replied. "In like five minutes, if we don't find it, we'll turn around."

I don't know why I listened to him.

I guess it's because, logically, I knew there wasn't much risk to driving around some weird neighborhood. It wasn't like we were wandering around in the middle of the woods, where we could get lost or die of dehydration or get eaten by a bear. It was one PM in the afternoon, and we were driving down a suburban road.

But the instinctual part of myself—the part that evolved over hundreds of thousands of years, that prevented humans from going extinct long ago—was screaming. *There is something wrong here. Get out. Get out, NOW.*

I drove forward, glancing in the rearview mirror. The stop sign lingered there, its bright red almost unnatural against the gray gloom of the sky.

Over the next few minutes, we didn't get any closer to finding Megan's house.

There were no street signs. No mailboxes. No indication of where we were going. Even the car's compass seemed messed up, as it switched from north to west a few times, even though we appeared to be going in a straight line.

"I'm just going to call Megan," Dave said finally, breaking the silence.

"Thank you," I snapped back, unable to keep the annoyance out of my voice.

After a moment, Dave shook his head. "Not picking up."

"All right, let's just go home."

"But we told her we'd be there!"

I sighed and stared at him. "Okay, so what do you want me to do? We're lost. GPS isn't working and she isn't picking up."

He paused, glancing around. "Maybe we should ask somebody."

"Who? There's no one here!"

"Maybe... knock on a door?"

My eyes widened. "That's... that's weird."

"Look, let's just knock on a door and ask. If they don't answer, we'll give up and go home."

I puffed out a breath. "Fine."

I pulled over to the curb. We got out and started up the driveway. It was no longer bright and sunny; the sky was a uniform, overcast gray. And the place was so... quiet. No voices, no cars passing by, no dogs barking. Just our footsteps on the pavement.

We walked up to the front door. When I didn't see a doorbell, I raised a fist to knock.

Thump, thump, thump.

No footsteps or barking from inside. "I don't think anyone's home," I told Dave.

"Just wait for a second."

"The address is definitely 52 Rosebud Lane, right?"

"I'm like ninety-nine percent positive, but I'll check." Dave pulled out his phone and scrolled. "Yep."

A minute went by. I knocked one more time. Then I leaned over and peered through one of the windows next to the door.

Wait... what?

The layout of the house was... really weird. The staircase was plopped in the middle of the foyer, with empty space on either side. Beyond it, in the kitchen, there was a floor-to-ceiling tower of cabinets. Not connected to a counter or anything, just *there*. There was a painting on the wall, of a woman standing on a rainy city street, but her eyes were drawn in upside-down.

What the hell?

It felt like I was looking at an AI-generated image. Something made by a machine, trying to replicate what a house was *supposed* to look like inside. Without any understanding of the function of stairs or cabinets or human behavior at all.

"Look," I said, motioning Dave over.

But he didn't share my sense of unease. Instead, he *laughed*. "Wow. Whoever designed these houses was an idiot," he whispered.

"Can we go now?"

"Yeah, okay."

We headed back towards the car. As I walked around to the driver's side, though, I felt the hairs on the back of my neck prickle. The familiar feeling of being watched.

I whipped around—but all I saw was the row of beige houses, staring down at me with their dark, shiny windows.

———

"We should be there by now."

"You must've just passed it up," Dave replied.

"No, we didn't."

It was almost 2 PM now. My stomach grumbled. My shoulders hurt. I just wanted to be back home, curled up under a blanket. Watching YouTube. Drinking tea.

We only made one turn. But somehow, retracing our steps, we hadn't intersected it yet. We hadn't even passed the weird stop sign. Nothing looked familiar, although of course *everything* looked familiar, because all the houses were the same house.

"It must just be up a little further."

"I just want to be home," I whined.

But a few minutes later, we passed something that we *definitely* didn't see on the way in.

A house that was different.

It was on the left side of the road. Everything about it was identical to the other houses—except for the porch railing. It was installed upside-down. Bolted into the underside of the roof, the banister at eye-level.

"What... the hell?" I asked, slowing down the car.

We both stared at the house. No builder or designer would make *that* kind of mistake. ...Would they?

A few houses down, there was another house that was different. This time on the right. Two of the windows had been connected into one long, 15-foot-tall window that extended from the ground to the roof.

"What the fuck?" Dave whispered.

"This isn't right," I replied, my heart pounding in my chest.

And then I saw it.

Just a few houses ahead of us was a mailbox. The only mailbox I'd seen on the street. And in small, gold lettering, were the words:

52 Rosebud Lane

Attached to the mailbox was a single pink balloon, fluttering in the wind.

"No. There's no way. It's not... it doesn't make sense."

There were no cars parked on the road. No voices or music coming from inside. No indication that there was a party going on except for that one balloon.

"I'm calling Megan."

The phone trilled in his ear. And then she picked up. "Dave! Where are you guys?"

"We're a little lost. We're in this development and…" He paused. "Do you have a pink balloon on the mailbox?"

"No," she said, confused. "It's the blue house on the hill. At the end of the cul-de-sac… did you turn on Mountain Ave.? It's a little hard to get here…"

She continued on, but I wasn't listening.

I was staring at the house.

Specifically, at the upstairs window.

Where a figure stood in the darkness, watching us.

I started the car and made a U-Turn, tires screeching against the pavement. Dave turned to me, eyes wide. "Someone's watching us. From that house." I stomped on the accelerator, the car rocketing down the suburban road.

"Slow down!" Dave shouted.

I glanced down. I was going 40.

"We can't—we have to get out of here—"

"You're going to crash, dammit! *Slow down!*"

But I did have to slow down.

Because up ahead, materializing out of the fog, was a stop sign.

This time, a cross walk.

And a cluster of school children crossing the road.

I stomped on the brakes. The car screeched to a halt. Dave and I jerked forward, the seatbelts locking us into place. My heart pounded in my chest.

Then I looked up.

And all the muscles in my body froze.

It wasn't a group of schoolchildren.

It was an amalgamation of arms and legs. Backpacks and sneakers. Tousled hair and ponytails. Put together like some nightmarish jigsaw puzzle. No faces, no eyes: just *things* that gave the allusion of a normal group of children crossing the street.

I stared at the monstrosity twenty feet in front of us, partially veiled by fog.

And then I switched the car into reverse.

"What the fuck—"

"Call 911!" I screamed at Dave. "*Now!*"

We careened past the upside-down railing, the 15-foot window, the pink balloon. As we sped by, the houses got stranger and stranger. Chimneys leading up to the sky. Floating gables. Hardwood floors that spilled out into the grass.

"They say they can't trace our location!" Dave shouted.

"Then—I don't know—tell them to go on the highway. Route 140. Turn at, at Glenmont Road, and then make a right at the subdivision."

He relayed that to them, but my heart was pounding. If we hadn't been able to retrace our steps... if they couldn't track our location... how would they find us?

I slowed down slightly. Glancing around the street, looking for something, *anything*, that I recognized.

But all I saw were the windows.

The curtains wide open, in every single one.

And people staring down at us. Although 'people' was a stretch—everything about them was *wrong*. Their faces had all the wrong proportions, stretched and misshapen. Their eyes were set in upside down. They had far too many hands.

People that looked like they had been crafted by some horrible AI.

Just like the houses they lived in.

———

It's now almost ten pm.

The sky should be dark. But it isn't. It's the same overcast gray color. We've made so many U-Turns, I've lost count. Back and forth, back and forth. But it's never the same. The houses, the people, are always different. Like the world is generating just for us each time we drive down it. Popping in and out of existence.

The police called us. They tried locating us, again and again. But every time they failed. They insisted there were only acres and acres of forest where we described our location.

I've used my phone to try to get other help. My parents tried to find us, too. Nothing has worked.

So I'm posting this online in the hopes that maybe someone, somewhere, knows how to escape this place. Maybe we'll finally get out. I'm so hungry. I'm so tired. All I want to do is stop the car and lie back in my seat, drift off to sleep.

But I'm afraid if I do that—*they'll* get us.

The not-people in the houses. They're learning. With each hour, they look more human. More like us. And they're getting bolder. I see children standing on the front lawn, still as statues. Women standing on the sidewalk, with faces that almost pass for human. Men crossing the street in front of us.

Whenever we drive by, they all start moving in our direction.

Like we're magnetic. A homing beacon.

Dave is driving now so I can post this. Maybe I'll take a short nap. For a brief moment, I won't be trapped anymore. I'll dream of being home, curled up with a cup of tea, watching TV with Dave. I'll escape this place, if only for an hour.

I'm signing off now. Hopefully someone out there, somewhere, knows how we can escape.

And if not, I'll have my dreams to comfort me for a little while.

I DELIVER LETTERS TO DEAD PEOPLE

I've been a mailman in Briarwood, Pennsylvania for almost a decade. In that time, nothing even remotely strange has happened. I just go to each house and deliver their mail while listening to podcasts. Sometimes I wave to the residents if they're outside. My job is probably the most stable thing in my life, to be honest.

But that all changed a few weeks ago.

That's when I started receiving the black letters.

At least, that's what I called them. They were envelopes that were pure black with silver lettering. No return address. No stamp, either, which was weird. They shouldn't have been able to get into my mail truck without a stamp. I didn't know what to do with them, but when I mentioned it to my boss, he seemed too busy to care.

So I delivered them with the rest of the mail.

I figured they were some sort of themed invitation

or something. Maybe a goth teenager's birthday party. Maybe even a funeral! I wasn't sure, and I didn't waste too much time thinking about it.

But then, more of them started appearing.

They all looked the same. A pure black envelope, with the same looping cursive. No stamp, no return address. I started feeling a little weird about it, because if they were invitations, they would've all been sent out at the same time. These were being sent out over the period of two weeks.

I was curious what was inside—but, of course, opening someone else's mail is a federal offense. So I didn't open them. I just continued delivering them.

Given that they were being sent out over the period of a few weeks, my theory changed. Maybe it was a new marketing campaign. Maybe for something goth or edgy, like a new Hot Topic or something. I don't know, I'm 35 year old single guy and have no idea what kids are into these days.

Eventually, around the 15th letter that I'd delivered, I recognized the name. Richard Fraser. He wasn't a friend or anything, but I'd run into him a few times. He was often walking his corgi around the cul-de-sac, and the dog would yap at me constantly. "I'm Richard, by the way," he'd said one day when I was delivering the mail. "Richard Fraser. I live up there." He pointed to a modern-looking house on the hill.

I slowed the mail truck as I came up to his mailbox. I stared at the silver lettering. RICHARD FRASER. 15 ROBIN CT... Shaking my head, I leaned over, popped open the mailbox, and slid it inside with the rest of the mail.

Two days later, Richard Fraser was dead.

I ran into his widow walking the dog. She looked very out of place: tall and thin, with a full face of makeup, stiffly walking after this wild, barking corgi.

I slowed the truck down. "Hi! Where's Richard?" I was actually hoping to ask him about the letter, if I could bring it up organically.

Her expression immediately darkened. "Richard... passed away," she replied.

She told me the whole story. He was in great health, great shape. But he'd had a brain aneurysm and suddenly died. Just like that. "Doctors can't really predict them," she said, her voice breaking. "So we had no idea..."

I didn't know what to say. I gave her my condolences and then drove away, continuing my route.

I didn't make the connection at that time. Between the letter and his death. He was an acquaintance I knew, and he passed away suddenly. It happens.

But then things started getting really weird.

A few days after I heard about Richard's passing, I got another letter addressed to him. It looked identical to the first one—black envelope, no return address or stamp, and looping cursive lettering. But there was one important difference: it had a different address.

Not 15 Robin Court, but 153 Elm Road.

I stared at the envelope in confusion. Richard

hadn't moved across town—he was *dead*. *Maybe that's his office address?* I thought. But I'd never seen any offices on Elm Road. It was a meandering road through the forest, scattered with a few single-family homes.

Why would this person send him two copies of the invitation, or whatever it was, anyway? And wouldn't they know he'd passed away by now?

I drove down Elm Road, dropping off various bundles of mail. When I got to mailbox number 151, I looked up, knowing the next house would be where I was supposed to deliver Richard's letter.

There was just one problem.

It wasn't a house.

It was the Briarwood Cemetery.

I pulled out my phone and typed in the address just to make sure. But it was correct—Richard's letter had been addressed to the cemetery.

And now, when I looked at the letter more closely, I noticed there was something written underneath the address line. The letters PL followed by the number 56. Could that be... plot number 56?

I pulled into the cemetery parking lot. Got out of my truck and began to wander through the cemetery. It took me 20 minutes, but then I was standing in front of a grave. The earth was freshly turned, and the name on the headstone read Richard Fraser.

I stood there for a moment, confused. If I hadn't seen any of the other black letters, I would've assumed a loved one was sending a letter to his plot. Maybe even a grandchild. Like a letter to Santa—a way for them to get their feelings out, to grieve. But why would someone send this black letter to Richard, find out he died, and then send another one to his grave?

It felt like some sort of morbid joke.

Not knowing what else to do, I set the letter against his headstone. Maybe whoever sent it would visit his grave and see that it had been delivered. I made a mental note, though, that if I saw any other letters addressed to 153 Elm Rd., I'd just give them to my boss and let him deal with it.

The next day, I found another black envelope in the mail. Not addressed to the cemetery, but to a house down by the lake. Addressed to a Breanna Chen. I didn't think much of it—until later that night, when I was browsing the local news and saw the headline: LOCAL WOMAN KILLED IN CAR ACCIDENT ON ROUTE 72.

Her name was Breanna Chen.

My blood ran cold. *No. There's no way.* I stared at the screen in front of me until the afterimage was burned into my eyes. *It's just a coincidence.*

But it was too much to be coincidence. I'd probably only handed out about twenty-five of these letters so far, and *two* of them had met sudden, untimely ends.

Lightning doesn't strike twice.

What about the others? There were a few other names I remembered, just because they were so ridiculous. Chrissy Feather. Steven King—with a V, instead of a PH. I googled both of them.

My stomach plummeted to the floor.

They were dead.

Chrissy had died of an anaphylactic allergic reaction, and Steven had been hit by a car while crossing the road.

I stared at their obituary pages, my heart pounding. *There's no way that's coincidence. The letters... they're somehow killing people.*

Or maybe just predicting the future?

First thing in the morning, I went to my boss and told him everything. That it seemed like everyone who received one of the black envelopes met an untimely death.

He laughed me off.

"It's just a coincidence. With 8 billion people in the world and so many things happening to them, there's bound to be some really weird coincidences. And what are we supposed to do, anyway? Stop delivering the mail?"

"I think we shouldn't deliver those letters. They don't even have stamps."

His face darkened. "They don't have stamps?"

"I told you that a few weeks ago. When I first told you about the letters."

He shook his head. "I didn't hear you, I guess. Sorry." Then he got up and started for the hallway. "Stan!" he called. "*Stan!*"

And then I was all alone.

Okay, so that was basically permission to remove all the black letters. Right? They didn't have stamps.

They never should've been allowed to get sorted into the mail in the first place.

That day, as I was making my usual route, I found two black letters. One addressed to Hector Garcia and the other addressed to Anna Ivanov. I slipped both in my pocket and continued like nothing had happened.

When I got home, I pulled out the letters. It felt *wrong*, having them in my house, on my kitchen table. *So what do I do with them now?* I thought. *Throw them out? Put them through the paper shredder? Burn them?*

Should I open them first?

I knew opening other peoples' mail was a federal offense. But if the envelopes had no stamps, were they really "mail"? Or were they just pieces of paper put into an envelope?

I grabbed the first one off the table, addressed to Anna. Held it in front of my face.

Then I ripped it open.

Inside was a folded, white piece of paper. I could see lines of ink through the underside of the page—but it wasn't writing. It almost looked like… a drawing? I flipped the paper open.

I froze.

It was a drawing of a woman, face-down in the lake.

For a second I stood there, frozen. Staring at the grotesque image. Someone had put a fair amount of detail into it—enough to draw identifying features, like a phoenix tattoo on Anna's left arm. Individual strands of hair, splayed out in the water.

I crumpled the paper in my hands. Crumpled it up

until it was a tiny little ball. Hands shaking, I grabbed the envelope addressed to Hector and ripped it open.

It, too, had a drawing inside. A drawing of car, barely recognizable with how crumpled and twisted it was. In the driver's side window, there was the silhouette of a man, head leaned against the steering wheel.

I crumpled it up too. Walked over to the trash— then thought better of it. *What if this whole thing becomes an investigation? What if someone finds these in my house? My garbage?* I walked over to the fireplace. Struck a match. Lit a roaring fire. Tossed the two crumpled pieces of paper inside, along with the envelopes.

The fire hissed and spit. More than it should've, for ordinary paper. It almost felt like the fire was angry at me. That there was something evil and horrible imbued in that paper, being burned up into ash.

I enjoyed the fire's glow for an hour afterwards, making a cup of tea and reading a book. Eventually, when the fire had gone out and I felt calm enough to sleep, I headed upstairs to bed.

For a few days, I didn't see any more black letters. Just the normal tide of ads and flyers and bills. I thought maybe this whole thing was over. Maybe somehow, not delivering the letters broke the curse or whatever it was.

But I was wrong.

On Tuesday morning, I found a letter addressed to Anna Ivanov. The woman in the drawing, lying in the lake. But her name, and her address, weren't written in silver cursive. They were written in jagged, angry red letters.

I can't deliver it.

I riffled through the other mail and sure enough—I found a second black envelope with red lettering, addressed to Hector Garcia. I pocketed both, and when I got to the park on Railway Ave., I pulled into the parking lot. Put on my hazard lights. Tore up the envelopes, without even opening them, and threw them in the trash.

I pulled out my phone and googled Hector and Anna. But no obituary or news articles popped up. *Maybe I prevented their deaths by refusing to deliver the letters.* That would be ridiculous, though, right?

Who's writing these letters, anyway?

Unless this person was also a serial killer, capable of killing not only with violence but with aneurysms and car accidents, I was dealing with something… different.

Something horrible.

I sucked in a breath and let it out. Then I pushed the thoughts out of my mind and pulled out onto the road, focused on my route. Things went fine, for the most part. The Doberman on Tulip Ave. barked at me a lot, but other than that, it was a peaceful day.

Until I got to the last bundle of mail.

There was another black letter that I'd missed. It

had been tucked in tight, wedged between two huge junk mail flyers. My heart pounding, my hands shaking, I slipped it out.

All the air sucked out of my lungs. It shook and fluttered in my hands, before falling to the floor.

Because it had *my* name on it.

For the longest time, I couldn't open it. I just sat there, watching the dying rays of sunlight out the windshield, flicking it back and forth between my hands. The silver lettering glinting against the black paper.

I knew what it would be. A grotesque, horrible depiction of my own death. And I couldn't open it—couldn't receive it. Opening it might cause my death—that seemed to be the case for Richard Fraser, Breanna Chen, and all the others.

I pulled back into the park. The cold wind, the babble of children playing on the nearby playground, all sounded muffled to me. As if I were underwater. As if they were in some faraway place, some happy place, completely disconnected from my own world.

Without opening the letter, I slipped it into the trash.

Then I delivered the final bit of mail, drove back to the post office, and went home.

I woke up later than usual the next day. My sleep had been interrupted; I kept waking up, over and over, for no apparent reason. *I should talk to someone about it,* I thought. *Talk to someone about the letters.*

I'd already told my boss, but his solution was just to not deliver the letters. I wasn't going to tell Rebecca—we'd only been seeing each other for a month, and I didn't want to freak her out or make her think I was some superstitious weirdo. I knew Dave would probably just laugh it off, but I decided I'd tell him about it this weekend when we met up for drinks. I had to tell *someone.*

Then I grabbed my coffee and rushed out the door. I got into my ice-cold car and slowly backed down the driveway. But, seconds later, I stomped on the brake.

My mailbox was hanging open.

There was something inside.

Not the usual mail. I hadn't *delivered* the mail yet. No, there was just a single letter—a single black envelope—inside my mailbox.

My heart dropped. I stopped the car and got out. Went over and pulled out the letter. No return address, no stamp. Someone had *hand-delivered it.*

And the writing wasn't silver. It was blood-red.

Just like Anna's and Hector's second letters. I swallowed, my throat dry. *They know. They know what I'm doing. That I'm getting rid of their letters.*

This is a threat.

I wasn't going to open it, obviously. Instead, I pulled back into the driveway. Put the car into park. Pulled out my phone. From here, I could access my doorbell camera.

Maybe it caught who delivered the letter.

I scrolled through the captured footage. 7:05 AM, there was motion detected—but that was just the school bus, picking up the neighbors. I tapped on the next one, taken at 5:28, but that was just a bug flying haphazardly around the porch. The next one had been taken at 3:42, and when I tapped play, my heart dropped.

For a few seconds, I just saw footage of my porch, with the dark, grainy shadows of the street beyond. But then, as I squinted at the screen, I saw something. A figure, tall and lean, approaching my mailbox from the left side of the screen.

No visible car or headlights. Just this figure, barely visible in the grainy footage, opening my mailbox. Slipping something inside. And then closing it.

For a moment, they paused. I couldn't tell if they were facing me, but it looked like they could be. Looking up at my house. Considering breaking in, maybe.

Then they continued on their way, disappearing off the right side of the frame.

Okay. It's time to call the police.

I had evidence of this person now. Delivering this weird letter. Mailing them all around town. Sure, you couldn't see their face or any details about them, but it was evidence. They couldn't dismiss me or tell me I was imagining things, or that it was a simple prank.

This person knew my address and came to my house in the middle of the night.

I shot off a text to my boss, and then called the police.

───────────

"Have you tried tracing the letters?"

Officer Martinez stared me down, hands crossed over her chest. She didn't seem very invested in all this, even though I'd just shown her video proof of this person. The black letter addressed to me remained unopened, sealed up in a little baggie in the middle of the table.

"You can't trace them. They don't have stamps, so they aren't marked or anything," I explained.

"And you don't have the other letters? The ones with the violent drawings, that you opened?"

"No. I... I threw them out." I knew lying to the police was bad, but I felt like telling her I burned them would make me look like I had something to hide.

"Well, I'd recommend setting up another camera on your mailbox, in case they do it again. It *is* technically against the law to put something in someone's mailbox like that." She locked eyes with me. "I'm going to take this back and open it now. Okay?"

I nodded.

She left with the letter. I couldn't help picturing what might be on the paper: a drawing of me, being stabbed by a faceless person in the darkness. Me, slumped against the steering wheel, in the tangled wreck of an automobile. Me, being chased down the street by that tall, dark figure...

Officer Martinez didn't come back for almost a half hour. When she finally did, she brought back the letter in a bag and held it up for me to read. It wasn't a drawing. It was just three words, all-caps, written in blood-red ink.

DELIVER THE LETTERS.

"Seems like this person is mad you didn't deliver their letters," she said. "I wouldn't be concerned about it. It's probably just some teenager playing some morbid prank. We've seen a lot worse from the kids around here, honestly."

"So you don't think I'm in any danger?" I asked.

"No, I don't think so," she replied. "But get a camera on the mailbox, so we can catch them."

"But all the deaths match up with the people who received letters," I insisted. "It's way too much to be by chance."

"Yeah, and I would be concerned if all those people died violent, unexplained deaths," she replied. "But as you said, Richard Fraser died of an aneurysm, and Breanna Chen died in a car accident. It's just a coincidence."

I thanked her for her time and left the police station. I got the feeling that she thought I was a scaredy cat, freaking out about nothing. I guess, in her service, she'd seen terrible things that some creepy letters couldn't hold a candle to.

But this was definitely the creepiest thing that happened in my peaceful little life, and I was terrified.

Teenager or not, this person knew where I lived. Who knows what they would do to me if I didn't deliver the letters. But if I did deliver the letters, more people might die.

I took the rest of the day off and bought a small camera. I attached it under the mailbox, where it couldn't be seen. Then I went to bed, hoping I wouldn't wake up to any footage of tall, thin, skeletal figures slipping letters into my mailbox.

Thankfully, there was nothing in my mailbox in the morning. I checked my footage, too, and there were no figures in the shadows. Nothing from the new camera, either. I went to work and told my boss everything, filling him in on my meeting with the police, the coincidental deaths, everything.

He told me to throw out any letter that didn't have a stamp, and that was it.

I got into the truck and started my route. I put on some music to help calm my nerves. I started at the north end of town, as usual, winding my way through the houses and clusters of forest.

But, unfortunately, my calm didn't last long. Because I saw another black letter, tucked away with in a bundle of cream and white envelopes.

Time stopped. I snatched it, brought it up to my face. My heart dropped when I saw the name: it was addressed Anna Ivanov again. The woman whose letter I destroyed, whose drawing showed her face down in the lake.

The address on this letter was different though.

It wasn't even a proper address. It just said, under her name, LAKESIDE DRIVE.

My blood ran cold. I quickly pulled out my phone and googled her name—but there was nothing about her online. No news articles, no obituaries, nothing.

The lump grew in my throat. I started the truck and headed towards the lake.

As I drove down Lakeside Drive, I studied the shoreline. Looking for a body. Looking for Anna. I finally pulled into the parking lot for the beach. It was eerie, roped off for the season, totally desolate. *Should I call my boss? Or the police? Someone?*

As I sat there, thinking, I saw it.

A dot of bright, neon pink in the distance. Bobbing up and down near the shoreline, about 30 yards away.

No. No, no, no...

I got out of the car and walked onto the shore. My boots sank in the sand. The cold wind whipped at my face. The neon pink dot grew closer in my vision. Deep down, I knew it was her. I knew it was Anna.

Even though I hadn't delivered the letters, she had succumbed to her fate.

I called the police. I couldn't get any closer without actually swimming out to her, so I just stood there, staring at the dot, until they arrived. When they did, I watched them swarm to her. They wouldn't tell me what was going on, but by their grim faces and their hurried tones into the radio, I knew.

I knew they'd found a body.

I slipped open the envelope. The one addressed to Anna, on Lakeside Drive.

It was just two words, written in jagged red letters.

I'M SORRY.

I didn't finish my route. I went home and shut the doors, locking myself in.

The only option was to quit my job. It was obvious. There was no other way out. I called Dave and told him everything, and he agreed with me. Surely the police would be taking the whole thing more seriously now, since they found Anna. But I didn't care. I just wanted out.

I couldn't fall asleep that night. I tossed and turned, thinking about the letters, about Anna in the water. *I should've warned her. I thought destroying the letters was enough. Why didn't I warn her? I knew where she lived. I could've knocked on her door.*

I can still warn Hector.

I looked up his number online. Dialed it around one am. He didn't pick up, because it was 3 AM, so I left a voicemail. I probably sounded delusional. But it didn't matter. I needed to tell him.

And then, just as I was about to fall asleep, my phone buzzed.

I picked it up—to see a notification.

A notification from the camera on the mailbox.

My blood ran cold. Hands shaking, I picked it up and tapped on the notification.

Nonono.

There was a face staring directly into the camera.

They were wearing a mask. A white, plastic mask with a sinister smile. The eye cutouts were pitch black, staring into the camera.

I dropped the phone. Then I ran over to the dresser and dragged it over my door. *I need to call the police.* I grabbed my phone off the floor.

The person was gone. I swiped away from the camera feed and started dialing 911.

Thump. Thump.

Footsteps.

Sounding right outside my door.

No. There's no way they got into the house that fast. I flattened myself against the wall furthest from the door. Staring at the doorknob, shining in the low light.

I pressed the phone to my ear. I was breathing so fast I felt lightheaded. "911, what's your emergency?" the operator asked, but her voice sounded so far away.

"There's someone in my house... someone right outside my door."

THUMP! THUMP! THUMP!

Three knocks on the door. It sounded like whoever was out there was trying to break down the door. The dresser rattled against the wood.

And then—the metallic, clicking sound of them turning the doorknob.

I ran into the closet. Pushed myself into the clothing, teetering on the boxes. I pulled the sliding doors shut in front of me, and then pressed my face up to the crack, peering out into my bedroom.

No.

The figure was standing in the middle of my room.

Like it had just passed through the door without any effort at all. It wore dark robes, cascading all the way to the ground. The white mask starkly contrasted with the shadows, frozen in that sinister smile. Eye sockets empty and blank.

"Hurry," I whispered into the phone. "It's in here with me."

But as soon as I said it, the masked face whipped towards me. Staring into the closet. My hand shot to my mouth. I held my breath.

It started towards me. But its head and shoulders barely moved with each step. It was almost like it was gliding towards me, across the bedroom floor.

I'm going to die.

That thought repeated in my head, over and over, as it got closer and closer. But then, just inches from the closet door—it stopped.

I watched as it pulled its hand from the folds of its cloak. Watched as its impossibly long, jointed, skeletal fingers lifted up towards its face. Its hand was as dark as its hollow eye sockets. Darker than its black robe—like its very being was the void itself.

There was something in its hand.

A letter.

The *thing* slipped the letter through the crack in the closet doors. With a fluttering sound, it bounced off my legs and fell onto the carpeted floor. I glanced down at it—and when I looked back up, the figure was gone.

I didn't come out of the closet, didn't move, until I heard the sirens. They searched the house, but I knew they wouldn't find it. Whatever that thing was... it wasn't of this world.

After they left, I walked back into my room. There, on the closet floor, was the letter. Except—it wasn't a letter. It wasn't an envelope. It was just a black piece of paper, from the same material as all the letters I'd received.

On the paper was a single sentence, in cursive silver scrawl. One sentence that made me realize I'd done everything wrong. That I hadn't understood the situation at all.

It read:

I WAS TRYING TO WARN THEM.

THE CURSED HOUSE

The realtor stared at me. "Are you *sure* you want to buy it?"

She'd told me everything. Apparently, the house was cursed. Every person who'd lived in it had died exactly one year later, to the day. In gruesome ways, too: Samantha Riley had slipped on the stairs and broken her neck. David Lu had gotten trapped in the basement and had a deadly asthma attack. Rebecca Jankowski had fallen through the attic window, thirty feet above the ground.

"Yes, I'm sure," I replied coolly.

"But every single person who's lived here has died in this house... exactly one year later. On the anniversary of the sale. Even with this price, we haven't been able to sell the house."

"I understand."

She was irritating me, now. Didn't she get it by this point? That I was buying the house *because* of the curse, not in spite of it? I briefly imagined her flopping down the stairs like poor Samantha Riley. At least that'd get her to shut up.

"You'd die on September 30, 2024," she continued, her face grim.

"I know."

"Only one more year of life."

"I know."

"The house is cursed. Don't you understand that?"

"Yes."

And then I did it. I lifted my hand and tugged at my hair. The wig slipped off easily, falling onto the table. She went white. Her eyes wide, her mouth open in a silent scream.

"I have three months to live," I said, gesturing to my bald head. "Stage four breast cancer. Metastasized to the brain, the lymph nodes, *everywhere*. If the curse really works—and I die *exactly* a year later—I'll be getting nine more months to live."

She stared at me, mouth agape. I picked a pen off the table and gave her a smile.

"I'm ready to sign."

More nightmares in my debut horror novel...

AVAILABLE NOW

I found an old childhood photo. There's something terribly wrong with it.

I found it in the back of my mom's closet. A photo of me, from when I was about 4. Except... the photo doesn't look *quite* like me. The eyes are too far apart. The grin is slightly too wide.

When I confronted my father, he wouldn't tell me anything. But then I found the old home videos. Which show a brother of mine, hiding in the shadows of the grainy film. A *twin*. A twin I don't remember, who my parents hid from me my entire life.

They say he's dead. A tragic accident, as a child. But I have a feeling he's very much alive.

And he's watching me.

Hungry for more horror? Visit www.blairdaniels.com or sign up for my newsletter.

Keep reading to learn about the inspiration behind some of the stories...

INSPIRATION BEHIND THE STORIES

I thought I would share the inspiration behind some of the stories—especially since a few of them are based in truth.

- *The Camera That Shows Your Last Photograph:* Inspired by realizing everyone has a last kiss, a last hug, a last meal, a last photo, etc.—but they don't know it at the time.

- *Be Careful What Your Kids Watch on YouTube:* The video described in the story is a real video my kids stumbled upon. You can find similar videos by searching "cocomelon wheels on bus sound variation" on YouTube.

- *There's Something Wrong With The Moon:* The moon appears rotated at different points throughout the night, and I only noticed this in my 30s. It still freaks me out.

- *The Headless Jogger:* I've been seeing people walking their dogs, or jogging, as late as 10-11 pm—and in the darkness, it's hard to see even the most basic of details. Like if they have a head.

- *Garden Hose:* I've been listening to a lot of Weird Al Yankovic lately, and the song "Hardware Store" has a lyric about garden hoses going for miles and miles. Really creepy, when you think about it...

- *I Let Something into My House:* My son, at age four, said some really creepy stuff. He actually said a lot of the dialogue in this story verbatim: "that woman has no face," "there's a man in the basement," "the woman is in the chimney." Super freaky stuff. I'm glad he grew out of that phase...

- *A Pyramid Scheme for The Dark Lord:* Inspired by reading a lot of posts on the subreddit r/antiMLM.

- *The Zmory:* I'm American, but Polish by ancestry, and I've been delving into Polish folklore. You can read about the Zmory here: https://lamusdworski.wordpress.com/2015/10/28/polish-mythology-zmory/

- *My Husband Wears People's Faces:* Sometimes, my husband says or does something random that reminds me of what an ex used to do. This story is about that feeling.

- *I'm Trapped in an Infinite Suburb:* Inspired by watching Backrooms footage, and the weird sterility of new construction homes. Seriously, those things feel more like a hospital than a home.

ALSO BY BLAIR DANIELS

DON'T SCREAM SERIES

Don't Scream

Don't Scream 2

Don't Scream 3

Don't Scream 4

TALES OF TERROR SERIES

You Can't Hide

Under Your Bed

Don't Look

Let Me In

NOVELS / NOVELLAS

Blood Twins

Attention, Shoppers

ANTHOLOGIES OF TERROR

Halloween Horrors

Terrors of the Forest

Daughters of Darkness

Printed in Great Britain
by Amazon